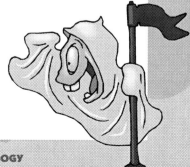

A YOUNG WRITERS ANTHOLOGY

First published in Great Britain in 2001 by
YOUNG WRITERS
Remus House,
Coltsfoot Drive,
Peterborough, PE2 192
Telephone (01733) 890066

All Rights Reserved

Copyright Contributors 2001

HB ISBN 0 75433 352 3
SB ISBN 0 75433 353 1

Foreword

Young Writers was established in 1991 with the aim to promote creative writing in children, to make reading and writing more fun. This year we received many ghost stories from our young writers of today and within these chilling pages we have brought you a selection of the very best.

The entries we have selected highlight the children's keen interest and enthusiasm for the creation of the short story and are a showcase of the writing talents of the future. Together they will chill your imagination with their frightful and often funny tales of the supernatural.

Read on for an irresistibly hair-raising experience that will keep you creeping back for more.

Steve Twelvetree,
Editor

Contents

The Curse of The Atttic	Victoria Masters	12
Dead Or Alive	Freya Scott	13
The Knife	Natasha Temple	14
A Ghost Story	Sarah Wainwright	15
The Teacher	Sophie Ruddle	16
The Moving Doll	Samantha Cheeseman	18
The Voice	Melissa Bye	19
In Loving Memory	Sadie Dudley	20
School Horror	Mark Hudson	21
The Unexplained Mystery	Darren Ackroyd	22
The House On The Hill	Charlotte Howard	23
Compelled	David Hartley	24
Rising From The Dead	Mark Rushton	25
Moving House	Oliver Jordan	26
The Ghost In The Street	Darren Bickley	27
The Big Crash	Siobhan Robertson	28
Dysfunctional Translucent	Daniel Byrne	29
The Ghost Of Thomas Kears	Andrew Fowles	30
That Little Stone Cottage	Charlotte Mann	32

The Haunting!	Laura Hindmarsh	33
The Mystery Ghost	Emma Holt	34
Theatre Fires Can Be Deliberate	Abram Welburn	36
Ghostly Behaviours	Charlotte Pennock	37
The Ghost Story	Kellie Dowson	38
Ghostly Thieves	Dylan Westwood	39
The Spirit Of Oakfield School	Antony Lockyer	40
Ghost Story	Christa Korsah-Brown	41
Mary, Mary Quite Contrary	Kathryn Elizabeth Callow	42
Miracle Treasure	Mehek Mushtaq	44
The Ghost Of Shallow Lake	Hannah Williams	46
Scream Dream!	Neha Jain	48
Jack The Ripper	Shareen Hearn	50
The Ghost That Wanted To Play	Aimee O'Reilly	51
The Black Knight	Daniel Monk	52
What?	Samantha Purvis	53
The Haunted Hamster At Hampton Court	Tessa Tyler Todd	54
The Evil Doll	Danielle Lilley	55
Echo Of The Past	Pippa Tess Bailey	56
Paint The Basement Green	Emma Dibley	58
Ghost In The Grand House	Katherine Cotterell	59
The Shadow Of Death	Sarah Beeby	60
The Hotel Murder	Amy Pollington	61
Terrifying Brother	Callie-Jo Hoover	62
The Lighthouse Mystery	Tom Bodley	63
Ruby Neckless	Amy Tosh	64

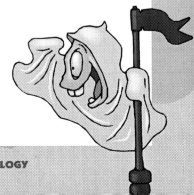

A YOUNG WRITERS ANTHOLOGY

The House On The Hill	Stephanie Lorraine Cressingham	65
The Ghost Of Watlington Church	Sophie Culley	66
The Graveyard	Abigail Baxter-Hunt	67
Ghost Story - Who's Out There	Kimberley Hurley	68
The Spirit Of The Valley	Lucy Jackson	69
Hardlock House	Crystal Whittick	70
Hardlock House	Mairah Akhtar	71
A Suspended Sentence	James Hancock-Evans	72
The Ghostly Atmosphere	Sarah Thorley	73
The Night Of Horror With Dadularr	Alex Cust	74
The Castle	Sarah Lamb	75
Ghost's Night	Cathy Seddon	76
The Haunted Doll	Alexandra Caddy	77
The Ghost In The Clock	Tejal Parmar	78
Your Wish Might Just Come True	Kimberley McTwan	80
Ghost Story	Alexandra Caulfield	81
Gateway To Hell	Caroline Marshall	82
My Horror Story	David Welton & Jonathan Williams	84
The Remains Of The Ghost	Lisa-Marie Sweeney	86
The Slimy Creature!	Philip Berners	87

Hallowe'en Night	Lana Montgomery	88
Dead Sleepy Hollow	Alexandra Pryce	90
My Scary Story	Frankie Narayan	92
Catastrophe Corridor	Jenny McKay	94
The Night Before Hallowe'en	Claire Emslie	96
Ahhh	Amy Gray	97
The House Of No Return!	Zoe Charge	98
The Disappearing Man	Ben Sayer	100
Beware!	Natasha Barnfield	101
The Haunted House	Amy Andrews	102
The Thing That Went Bang In The Night	Charlotte Robertson	104
The Haunted Swimming Pool	Lauren Agambar	105
The Illusions	Jake Skinner	106
The Mystery	Jessica Adams	107
The Illusion	James Hackney	108
The Missing Person	Samantha Miller	109
Untitled	Spencer Eve	110
The Hunger	Pietro James Catalano	111
The Babysitter's Ghost	Karen Evans	112
Devil's Hall	Rachel Thompson	113
The Executioner	Leah Anne Eades	114
The Orphan Ghost	Amy Innes	115
Never Disturb A Ghost	Sarah James	116
Recurrence	Stacey Dunn	117
Hallowe'en Special	Kathleen Ingleby	118
Cut	Claire Warren	119
The Haunted House	Jade Nugent	120

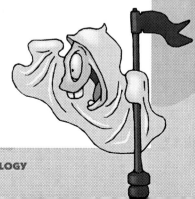

A YOUNG WRITERS ANTHOLOGY

The Ghost Hunter	Vanessa Hodgson	121
The Victorian Orphanage	Dominic Skuratko	122
The Blood Cut Finger	Jessica Young	123
The Ghosts Of Spooksville Castle	Jessica Lawson	124
The Haunted House	Andrew Jamieson	125
Death Cottage	Alex Rae	126
The Forbidden Garden	Amy Craddock	127
Friday The 13th	Cheryl Smith	128
The Blood Bat	Emma Humphries	129
Three Girls And An Island	Chelsea Lawrance	130
Haunted Castle And The Vampire Aunt	Stephanie Pereira	131
What Will Happen Next?	Sarah Anderson	132
Haunted House	Vanessa Broadbent	133
Search For Her Son	Christopher Graham	134
Clair's Spooky Experience	Sharon Royle	135
Terror Cottage	Sean Andrews	136
Ghost Stories	Glen Middleton	137
The Story Of Geoffrey Cook!	Caroline Blackwood-Wallace	138
The Hitchhiker Ghost	Zoe Hutchinson	139
The Boyfriend	Laura Fannan	140
The Haunted Hotel	Jennifer Ash	141

Dead Man's Den	Lee Collinson	142
A Mother's Vision	Lauren Arnison	143
Death On The Moulin Rouge	Lauren Sutherns	144
The Awakening Of The Dead	Stephen Dickerson	145
Insomnia Or Death?	Danielle Miller	146
Who's That	Laura Preston	148
Full Moon Scare	Jamie Ross	149
The Winter's Night	Benjamin Jobson	150
Dead Spells	Jonathan Norris	151
The Stalker	Scott Brown	152
The Screaming Sewer	Iain Fawcett	153
Drip, Drip, Drip	Mark Allison	154
Saxon Curse	Kayleigh Thompson	155
What Is Underneath	Laura Allen	156
The Ghost	Erin Taylor	157
The Haunted Staircase	Nicole Carman	158
A Dream	Josh Mannix	159
Jail Boy	Toby Burraway	160
Scary Waters	Lauren Allen	161
The Den In The Haunted House	William Tate	162
Sweet Dreams	Angharad Seabury	163
Lord Townby Vs Lady Townby	Clare McLoughlin	164
The Ghost Story	Jordan Rutherford	165
A Night In The Adersons' House	Stephanie Hennerbry	166
The Haunted House	James McKenzie	168
The Scare!	Courtney Green	169
A House	Samantha Short	170
The House On Cherry Hill	Charlotte Bebbington	171

A YOUNG WRITERS ANTHOLOGY

Jasper The Funny Ghost	Lisa Telford	172
Bottled Out	Richard Gilbert	173
Help	Rachel Chilcott	174
Hardlock House	Jodi Riggan	175

The Stories

A YOUNG WRITERS ANTHOLOGY

The Curse Of The Attic

Jennifer clambered up the steep, dark stairs. She could hear footsteps running in a desperate manner, as if running from someone or something . . .

Suddenly, the story of the murdered girl twenty years ago, in this very attic flashed back into her memory. Was this a re-enactment of the mystery?

As Jennifer was thinking this through, her classroom door slammed shut, leaving her outside; she had to enter. The door creaked open, to reveal nothing. She screamed with fright, as the door once more slammed behind her.

Suddenly, the old balcony door shut. This was very puzzling, as it hadn't been opened for twenty years. A feeling of déjà-vu flooded over her. The balcony seemed to hold a dark secret. As this became clear to her, an axe man appeared from the shadows, and walked menacingly towards her. The secret was that the axe man had to kill someone, every twenty years. Tonight was the night. Jennifer had been the little girl, who was murdered here twenty years ago. The axe man was back, to retake her life.

She edged towards the door, horror stricken. She peered into his evil eyes. Jennifer fled from the attic and down the staircase. A scream followed her down the forbidden stairs, a scream that would haunt her all her life, the scream of her previous self again taunted and once more killed by the axe man's sharp, well-used blade.

But at least it wasn't her present life that she lost: this time.

Victoria Masters (12)

Dead Or Alive

'BBC! Radio Two, hello and welcome to the ten o'clock news. A man called John Thaw died this afternoon at Newberry Prison for mentally ill men. The public has been warned to keep an eye out for any mysterious goings on, since several men reported seeing him after his time of death.'

'Mark, I don't feel safe driving out here in this wilderness, with the nearest village four miles away and the fuel tank almost empty.'
'What?' Mark shouted jerking out of a trance.
'The fuel tank,' repeated Helen, 'it's almost empty.'

As she finished her sentence the engine stuttered and died.

'Oh!' Mark swore. In a rage he turned round and grabbed the torch from the back seat, got out of the car and walked off into the darkness, leaving Helen all alone.

Three hours later, Mark still hadn't come back and Helen was worried. She turned the radio on to Steve Wright, but instead she found a news report about a murder a mile out of the village, but when the police had got there the body had gone.

Suddenly something started banging on the roof and at the exact same moment Helen's heart started banging against her ribs. Then a knife came against her ribs. Then a knife came plunging through the roof cutting Helen's right cheek. She screamed and leapt out of the car. As she turned around, there was her husband with the knife and the ghost of the dead man behind him, grinning. She ran, and after a while she fell down dead.

Freya Scott (13)

The Knife

I looked out of the window and heard the wind whispering to the trees. Suddenly I heard a creak, what was that? I thought, should I get up?

I ventured out of my warm bed. What if it was a burglar? I thought, maybe I should phone my parents.

As I tiptoed down the stairs, the phone started ringing. I ran back into my room to answer it.

A man's voice spoke into the phone, 'Come downstairs.'
'What, who, who is this?' I whispered.
'Never mind, just come downstairs or I'll come up and get you' he replied.

I looked out of the window, I peered out of my door. He was watching me, calling me, telling me to go downstairs, so he could kill me. If I didn't go, he'd come up.

I walked slowly down the stairs, trembling with every step. I saw a shadow of what I thought was a man but as he got closer I realised this wasn't a man, this was a ghost, a ghost with a knife.

I screamed as he lunged towards me and plunged his dirty knife into my flesh. There was a huge thud and I was gone, gone for ever.

Natasha Temple (12)

A Ghost Story

As I woke up, my head beamed with pain, I tried to sit up, but even my strength was no match.

I reached up to feel my forehead, and my hair was damp. Sweat trickled down my cheek bones and dripped on to my pillow. My knees were trembling within my sheets, yet I was relieved to be well.

I had just been somewhere! I had been into the wonders of the Earth, and never more do I intend to go there again . . .

I was walking through mist and fog when I saw her, just hanging there. Was she real? She looked it! There was a thick rope held tightly around her neck. Her face had turned blue and her eyes had swollen. Though she was smiling, her black teeth were looking at me amongst the mist.

Above her, I saw a star shape. On each corner was a figure; at the time I couldn't see who, but they too were as dead as the earth and just staring at me, through the disturbing night.

I began to run away, though it seemed the further away I ran the closer they got. My head was spinning, my eyes were blurry and watery, and my pupils had shrunk so small they were hardly noticeable. And then, my eyes blacked out. When I awoke it seemed that nothing had happened; it couldn't have all been a dream, could it?

Sarah Wainwright (14)

The Teacher

'Why is Mrs Leech stroking her arm? Amy asked Tom.
'That's her dragon bite!' said Tom mysteriously.
'You really think I'm gonna believe that?'
'It's the truth' argued Tom. Amy shook her head and carried on with her work.
'Pens down' demanded Mrs Leech, 'we're now going to do an experiment, we're going to examine lizards.'
'What's the point?' mumbled Amy.
'So she can be at peace with her ancestors!' Tom joked, and they both started laughing.
'What was that Tom?' shouted Mrs Leech.
'Nothing.'
'Good. Now pair up and collect a lizard from the jar' ordered the batty old teacher. Mrs Leech was an old woman who spent her time being cruel and devious to children, if you went trick or treating at her house, all you would get is a menacing look and the door slammed in your face.

'Look at Mrs Leech, she's stroking the lizard and, look' said Amy. Tom looked up at Mrs Leech.
'Her eyes are turning completely black and her skin is turning scaly' shouted Tom.
'Children it's time for lunch!' cackled Mrs Leech.

The children were screaming, they had heard the rumours, but never actually believed that Mrs Leech was a child-eating dragon. Mrs Leech's skin had turned orange, her nails had sharpened, her teeth were now yellow, her arms had turned into enormous wings and a long black tail had grown out of her back.

Tom turned to Amy, 'What if we open the blinds and, uh, maybe the sun will kill her.'

Amy stared at Tom and said, 'Tom, A, there are no blinds in this room. B, she's a dragon not a vampire and C, it's December, there is no sun, only rain, you're an idiot!'

'Say that again?' asked Tom.

'You're an idiot,' said Amy.

'No! You said there's only rain. Why don't we use water instead of the sun?' said Tom.

'That might work, maybe she never goes near water, in case it takes her power away forever?' said Amy.

'Well it's worth a try, turn on the tap, cover it with your finger so it will spray all over her.'

Amy ran to the other side of the classroom, and reached the tap, but so did Mrs Leech. She hit with her tail and knocked her so hard she fell unconscious on the floor. Tom ran over immediately and broke the tap; water came pouring out all over Mrs Leech. Her skin started smoking, she gave a last yell then completely vanished leaving only her bones on the floor.

So if you ever see any old animal bones in your school biology lab, you can bet Mrs Leech haunts them.

Sophie Ruddle (13)

The Moving Doll

It was school, school once again, we went out into the playground to play hide and seek as usual. My friend Leah and I went to hide together in the same place as we always did. We were hiding, hiding behind the bit of broken fence near the house that everybody liked, it was really posh. We always looked up at the window with the beautiful China doll in it.

When suddenly it moved and started walking. We thought it was the lady who owned the house mucking about, but then we looked at the house and saw her downstairs so the doll must be a ghost of someone.

It was time to go in. We didn't tell any of our other friends about it, but every time we went to hide we always hid there, no one ever found us. The China doll always did the same thing, walked on the window sill, but one day the window was open where the doll was.

She got blown out of the window and said to us, 'I'm going to watch you all the time, I can see you everywhere and know what you're saying.' We didn't believe it, but when we started talking about it the doll said, 'I can hear you!'

At this time we believed the doll was a ghost. We moved our hiding place and millions of China dolls surrounded us. We shouted for *help* but nobody else could see them. After that day every time we went to hide the dolls came. But then the lady did the decent thing and chucked the doll away and nothing happened ever again.

Samantha Cheeseman (13)

The Voice

It was a damp winter night, murky and bitterly cold. She had been left alone while her father was out of town in a draughty, decrepit old house. All day she had sat on the sofa hugging a cushion with her eyes closed, so scared of the night, but soon it came.

The grandfather clock chimed eleven, it made her jump. She closed the lounge window tightly, drew the curtains so no light peaked through a gap. Then one by one, slowly and carefully she checked every window in the house, making sure twice they were closed. Her heart pounding she picked up her candle, hand a-shaking. Nervously she took one last thorough look around the house. She sighed in relief when she found that nothing was there.

She climbed the creaking stairs and locked herself in her cold, damp bedroom. She peeled back her heavy cotton sheets and slipped between them quickly. She lay shuddering for a few moments before the one candle lighting the room burned itself down to the bottom of the wick and extinguished itself.

'That's nice,' said a sinister, crackling voice, 'now we're tucked in for the night.'

Melissa Bye (14)

In Loving Memory

Sandra was told she could never get pregnant so she decided to adopt a baby girl, she called her Sadie. Then a couple of years later, when Sadie was two years old, Sandra became pregnant and she had a baby boy, she called him Shaun. He was very poorly when he was born and the nurses did not look after him properly. He was so poorly that he died at the age of six days. Then Sandra got pregnant again with another boy, she called him Ian and he was fine.

Sadie and Ian grew up, Sadie was ten and Ian was eight years old. They were at school one Monday and Sandra was at home in Ian's room tidying up. It was dinner time, so she went and made some dinner. Sandra went back into the bedroom to carry on tidying up and she saw a white feather, she went to pick it up but it disappeared, so she went for a walk because she felt sad. She walked to the top of a hill and sat down on a bench.

She shouted Shaun and then she saw him in the distance. He waved and then disappeared. But after seeing him she felt happy because she knew that he was safe. So she went home and she walked through the door and there was a white feather again so she went and picked it up and this time it did not disappear. Three years later she has still got the feather in a cabinet.

Sandra felt that he wanted to say goodbye and love you loads Mum, Dad, Sadie and Ian.

Sadie Dudley (12)

School Horror

Jim and his friends went upstairs to finish off their work. The bell went, his two friends ran down the stairs. Jim shouted, 'Wait.' He ran after them but tripped and died.

Thirty years later Mr Burns, the headmaster shouted, 'Right I have had enough of you three kids, first smashing the window and locking the maths teacher, Mrs Lees, in the stock cupboard. I am ringing your mums and telling them to come in and pick you up at 5pm.'
'Why?' said Jack.
'Because you are having an after school detention' said Mr Burns.
'You're joking' said Matt.
'Does it look like I am joking?' shouted Mr Burns.

At 3.30pm the bell went. Jack, Matt and Oliver went to the head's office. He was talking to the three children when the secretary walked in and said, 'Right I am going, will you be alright on your own?'
'Yes' said Mr Burns.

Mr Burns was talking when a voice shouted, 'I am Jim, the ghost of this school. I died thirty years ago and now you will die.'
Mr Burns looked at the children and said, 'Quick run out the door.'
Jack tried to open it. 'It's locked!' he said.
The voice shouted, 'You'll never get out of here.'

Then suddenly they heard a car drive up. They tried opening the door. It was unlocked, they ran out.

As Matt was going home he thought he must have imagined it but he didn't!

Mark Hudson (12)

The Unexplained Mystery

The school summer holidays had just started and Tracy was going to visit her grandma who owned a hotel. The hotel lay on the hills of Scotland.

Tracy's grandma knew that the house was haunted and warned Tracy straight away. She took no notice of her grandma at all. That same night there was a rattling sound coming from a bedroom which was shut off because someone had died in it and they were scared of any haunting in it. Tracy went up to examine it. The whirring sound of wind coming out of the windows made it quite scary.

Tracy opened the door and the room was full of cobwebs. Very mysteriously there were some strange letters and signs on the walls of this room. The light flickered on and off and the door banged shut. Tracy's heart was in her mouth as she was looking round the room. She was screaming for help but there was no answer. Tracy's grandma remembered that when Tracy was younger, her elder sister died in the room but Tracy was too young to remember that.

She screamed and screamed but there was still no answer. Her grandma wondered where she had got to and started looking around the hotel. She looked in her diary and saw that it said that she had gone into the room, but where was the door? There was just a wall. Tracy was never seen again.

Darren Ackroyd (13)

The House On The Hill

It was a cold, rainy night and as lightning struck it lit up the house, which stood on top of the hill.

A man approached the house vigilantly and wrapped his hand around the cold, brass door handle, the door creaked open and the man walked slowly into the dark house.

At the far corner of the room were some stairs. The man walked up the staircase, which creaked as he went. Lightning struck making the man stop in alarm. When the lightning stopped the man carried on walking up.

When he was at the top he came to a door. He slowly opened it but the room was cold, dark and empty so he came out, closing the door behind him.

The wind was wailing outside and in the distance he could hear the sound of a werewolf howling. The man saw another door that was slightly ajar so he went to investigate.

The man walked into the room and just as he did lightning struck, lighting up the whole room. The man looked around and noticed a small, sinister figure crouched by the wardrobe.

As the man walked over he could tell the figure was that of a young boy. He looked down and the small, pale boy looked up and said, 'You've found me Daddy, now it's your turn to hide!'

Charlotte Howard (13)

Compelled

The rotting door flung open in front of her. She didn't want to enter the grand house, she didn't even want to go near it, but she couldn't help it, she was driven there by a greater force than curiosity and she couldn't do anything to stop it.

Her feet dragged her into the room and the light dimmed. Frightened of what the dark could drag out of her imagination, she stepped to the curtains that blocked out light, each hand gripped a curtain, she breathed deeply and pulled. Her heart slammed against her chest as if it were trying to escape, she uttered a gasp as her eyes beheld . . . a tree. The branches of the tree scratched the window, another leaf surrendered and floated to the ground. She sighed and took more deep breaths as she backed away from the light that now streamed through the window.

Her feet carried her body through the doorway of the room and took her down the corridor. She could see another room at the end of the hallway that contained one solitary item, a child's rocking horse and it was rocking. She was compelled towards it until she stood only inches away and she reached out to stop it moving. Her hand met the smooth, crafted shape of the horse's nose and the rocking ceased, the house was silent again, and, as the breeze swept through the open door and the tree scratched a final time she turned and looked. She screamed.

Daivd Hartley (15)

Rising From The Dead

Joe was going home after a long day at work when he ran out of petrol. He saw a house and knocked on the door. An old lady answered and Joe asked if he could use the phone. The old lady said that she didn't have a phone but that Joe could stay there if he wanted.

They were sitting down chatting. The lady told Joe that her husband had died and that she lived alone. Joe commented on a ring on her finger, Joe liked the ring. The lady told Joe to sleep on the sofa.

Joe was woken by someone moving around. He went upstairs and there was no one there. He went into the lady's room, he couldn't believe his eyes! There was no roof and the floorboards were broken. Nothing was there! Nobody had lived there for ages. What was going on? *Crash!* He fell through the floor.

He had fallen into the lady's hands! She saved his life! She told him that she had accidentally locked herself in the cellar and that she had starved to death. Her ring was in the bedroom and if I could find it and put it on her finger she could rest. Joe went upstairs and the room was back as it used to be! There was the ring. He ran down to the cellar and put the ring on her finger. She said, 'Thank you' and vanished.

Mark Rushton

Moving House

Everyone was up, the lorries were packed. We were moving. The journey was a long one. When we arrived it was getting quite dark. The house was in the middle of a wood in the countryside of Shropshire. The lorries were all unpacked; Bill, Ben and myself took a look around the big house.

'It's time for bed' Mum said, 'we are going shopping tomorrow to Harry Tuffins to get some paint.'

Bill and Ben slept in the same bedroom and I slept on my own. I woke up in the night thinking there was someone looking over me but there wasn't, there was a cold draft and the bedroom door banged.

We started painting the house but things kept on moving. We couldn't find the paint pots. They were not where we had left them and the paint on the walls had changed colour overnight. We were feeling frightened.

Weeks later the house was looking more cosy. Mum and Dad thought they would invite their friends over for a meal and to stop the night. The meal was disgusting. We opened a bottle of wine, it was the same. It was midnight, the music changed from jazz to old-fashioned music. We tried to open the doors and the windows but they were stuck solid. There was a reflection of an old woman in the mirror. Dad picked up a chair and threw it at the window and a voice was shouting, 'You will never get out, I've got you.' But the window smashed, we all jumped out and ran for our lives.

Oliver Jordan (13)

The Ghost In The Street

There was a boy called Matt. His friends went to Matt's house. They went there because Matt said he had a ghost in his house.

They went to look at Matt's house and, sure thing, there was a ghost up in the attic. There was an old box going around the room. Matt's girlfriend had followed them up there. She was scared, she started to scream. The box fell onto the floor. Matt's mum called him, 'Come down out of there now.'
Matt said, 'In a minute.' Matt said to his mate, Ben, 'Come and call for me later and we will have a look.'
Matt's girlfriend said, 'You are so brave.'

So the same night Will and Ben came back, but when they got to the attic there was nothing there. No boxes, nothing. Where had they gone? Then Ben said, 'Can you hear that screaming?' They went downstairs and went outside. Matt's girlfriend was screaming. She said she had seen a ghost by all the boxes outside. Then there was another scream. They all went running around to the boxes. There was the ghost. Matt's mum was there now.

He seemed to be looking for something, so Ben went and tipped all the boxes on the floor and the ghost picked up something. It looked like an old clock. It must have been Matt's great-granddad coming back to collect the old clock from the house where he used to live.

Darren Bickley (13)

The Big Crash

Sally was going to a party and she had to be back by 11 o'clock. Her dad said he would come to pick her up.

When the time came her dad failed to arrive, so she carried on waiting. By then it was 12 o'clock, so she decided to walk home.

She was walking along the roadside when a car drove by. She was expecting it to be her dad but it wasn't. Already several cars had passed her and she started to wonder where her dad was. Just at that moment her dad came round the corner. She tried to stop him. When he got by her side he stopped and just as quickly as he appeared he disappeared. This frightened Sally and she ran home as fast as she could. The police had to break the news to Sally's mum and when she got home her mum gave her the bad news that her dad had died.

The police were at her house and they said that they were going to investigate how her dad had died.

They did the investigating and found out that someone had been fiddling with her dad's brakes on his car and that is what caused the crash.

'Who did it?' asked Sally.
The policeman said, 'I don't know, but we will find out.'

They did more investigating and decided that he had done it himself. Sally and her mum would always wonder if he had deliberately killed himself or whether it was an accident?

Sally knew that he had come to see if she was alright on her way home.

Siobhan Robertson (13)

Dysfunctional Translucent

The night was dark; and the mist had descended over the old cemetery. As I walk through the darkness, I cannot see more than a few metres in front of me while I search for the grave of my beloved. Suddenly, I heard a crack behind me. When I turned around there was nothing but darkness. I carried on walking, still glancing over my shoulder, before turning back to look where I was going, and there it was - a huge wolf, maybe a werewolf. Its teeth as huge as an elephant's tusks, a snarl as loud and frightening as thunder. I froze on the spot, not knowing what to do. Should I run and risk being chased, or stay and pray for a miracle?

All of a sudden, something came over me and before I knew it, I was running away in a mad dash for my life. I could hear the beast catching up with me. I could see the cemetery gates up ahead, but I knew I wasn't going to make it. The overpowering force of this thing's weight took me down. It tore chunks out of my flesh like I was a soft cushion; before tearing out my guts which it ate immediately.

It took my life that night. All I can do now is walk among the dead as a dysfunctional translucent, waiting for the beast's bloodline to be broken. Time has gone on - many more have died; yet the bloodline continues to exist.

Daniel Byrne (16)

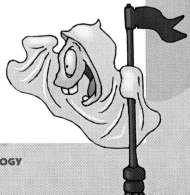

The Ghost Of Thomas Kears

12th November 1850

Thomas Kears watched in sheer terror and screamed a stricken scream as Dr Solit raised his knife above his prone body. He closed his eyes and waited . . . 'Aarrh' he cried in pain. He took a quick glimpse at the knife wound and his life's blood draining before his very eyes.

18th July 1999

'Darling, come here, I need your help to strip the wallpaper' shrieked Mum.
'Coming.'
'Oh hello my name's Andrew Kears. We've just moved into an old mansion of a house. My parents inherited it from my grandma.'
'Andrew, come here quick' cried Mum.
I ran upstairs knowing this wasn't just any wallpapering job.
'I was just taking the wallpaper off' explained Mum.
'When you found a door leading to a room' I butted in.
'Yes.'
I stared around the room, just a look at the place gave me the creeps, it was so empty . . . and cold.

12th November 1999

I raised my arm in fear and opened the oak door leading to *'the room'*. I needed to find out where those noises were coming from. I gritted my teeth and stepped in. Everything seemed normal, I was just about to go when a piece of paper blew off the table. I froze, scared. Suddenly the door slammed shut. I felt faint.
'I'm free' said a booming voice.
'Www what do you want' I

murmured.
'Just get me to Dr Solit's grave for he was the one that murdered me, Sir Thomas Kears, in this very room.'

Too scared not to obey I quickly took him to the graveyard.
'Thank you Andrew, your work is done.'
'Tttt thank you.'
Quickly I sprinted back home, not wanting to experience what was in store next.

Andrew Fowles (11)

That Little Stone Cottage

'Today we're going to look at the stone cottage where witches were said to have burnt an innocent girl, who still roams the woods at night.'
'Come off it,' I said.
'Suit yourself!' John replied. 'And this . . . is the cottage.'

The trees surrounding the cottage stood silent after the storm. The wet, green leaves looked beautiful as the first rays of sunlight caught them. I looked up at the crumbling stone building, half covered in ivy. A shiver went down my spine. There was still evidence of the fire, despite the renovation work carried out by John. I stood there looking at it, while the others moved on. Something caught me.

Later on in the day I was still curious about the house, so I went inside and was startled by a woman, just sitting there. 'I'm Amelia.' I just nodded. 'Don't worry, I'm John's wife.'
'Of course' I said, deeply relieved. We talked for ages, then I was heading back to my tent when I saw smoke rising from the forest. 'Oh no!' I gasped, as I started running. As I approached the cottage I heard screams coming from inside. I followed them until I found Amelia.

'Come on!' I said as I reached out to grab her, but I stumbled and fell over, holding thin air.
'I'm sorry' she said.
I was screaming. Flames appeared in the doorway as I started towards it, it slammed shut. I stepped backwards as the hay beneath my feet caught fire and the smoke choked me. My eyes rolled back as I fell to the floor.
'Amelia . . .' I said, but she was gone.

Charlotte Mann (14)

The Haunting!

'Ahhh!'
'What is it Lucy?'
'Sorry! I thought I heard something strange in our elegant Georgian mansion.'
'Well, what did it sound like darling?' asked Joshua.
'Oh well, there were two noises, one was a 'whoo' and then there was a loud crash.'
'Oh well, it was probably your imagination dear, go back to sleep.'

Next morning in the new house, Lucy went down the grand spiral stairs and saw a door.
'Strange I've never seen that door before.'

She walked over and opened the door, it squeaked loudly. She walked in and saw another door, she tried hard to open it but it was locked.

She looked around and on the dusty floor was an old rusty key, she picked it up and slotted it carefully in the keyhole, she turned the key slowly and opened the door. As she opened it, the other door with a dull thud - closed.

She ran to it and banged and tried to kick the door down but it was well and truly stuck.

Then suddenly something crept out of the other door and silently stole up behind her, it caught hold of her round the waist and dragged her roughly, kicking and screaming into the other room.

That's when she turned round and realised, it was her previous rich husband.

'What are you doing here? said Lucy, terrified.
'I came to make your life a misery, like you made mine.'
'But why?'
'Because you and Joshua murdered me!'

Laura Hindmarsh (10)

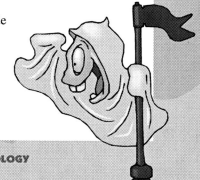

The Mystery Ghost

We walked into the churchyard. Jack and I crept up to the church house. Creek, thud, thud, thud. 'What was that?' I whispered.

'I don't know!' whispered Jack 'Quick behind the tree.' Dong, dong, dong. Suddenly a shadow appeared it seemed to be moving.

'It's a ghost!' Jack said,
'Oh don't be silly Jack.' I said 'it's not a ghost.'
'Oooh!' said something.
'Aaah!' we shouted.
Then bang, crash! 'It's a ghost' I said 'quick run!'

We ran past the church and into the bush by the lake and waited until the noises faded into the darkness.

The next day we went back to the old church house, determined to catch the mystery ghost.

That night we waited until 3 o'clock and we heard the same noises. Bang, crash! Oooh! We saw the shadow appear.

Jack and I both had nets to catch the ghost.

1, 2, 3 *Wham!* Jack caught the ghost, Jack lifted up the net to reveal the ghost.

'Hang on a minute, this is not a ghost!' I said 'it's Mr Smith, the church warden.'

'We thought you were a ghost' explained Jack.
'Oh no! I'm not a ghost!' Mr Smith said.
'But what about the big bang?' questioned Jack.
'Oh that was just me cutting wood' he said.

'And what about the *'ooooh'* then' asked Jack.
'Oh that was my owl Percy. Oh you two have got into a muddle' he said.
'Come on! I'll show you Percy!'

Emma Holt (10)

Theatre Fires Can Be Deliberate

It was Friday night and everyone, well at least it seemed like everyone was going to see the big show at the Royal Theatre. When eventually I got in, the lights dimmed and the curtains opened to reveal a man dressed smartly in black and white. He said 'Hello! I'm Mr Johnson tonight you will see a number of shows from countries around the world such as Germany, France and . . .' But just then, the curtains began to close. 'Whatever is the matter?' exclaimed Mr Johnson and went off to investigate but found nothing.

'Oh well! There's nothing there' he said 'so I'll carry on. Well where was I. Oh yes that's it! Germany, France and the USA! But first we will see the Grimaldi Circus from Italy . . .' but the curtains began to close for the second time.

'This is ridiculous!' said Mr Johnson 'absolutely ridiculous.' But then the curtains began to open. So Mr Johnson thought nothing more of it, just as the actors were coming on, a thin whisp of white smoke floated to the back of the theatre, or was it smoke?

All of a sudden, the back curtain was engulfed in flames and every person in the theatre ran for their lives, but about six people got caught in the rising flames. 'Fire, fire!' People were shouting as they ran out of the theatre door but as the last person pushed her way through the door, she took a last glimpse over her shoulder and saw a ghostly figure engulfed in flames laughing at what he had done!

Abram Welburn

Ghostly Behaviours

I knew as soon as I walked into that room that something wasn't right, it didn't quite fit into place.

Even seven days later when the room had been decorated, it felt cold. I decided to paint it red so it wouldn't feel so cold, I was wrong!

One day I walked in there and my favourite vase was smashed, the room started shaking and the walls turned to *blood!* I fell against the wall, my mind was whirling with different thoughts, the ornaments were dropping like flies. 'What could I do?' I yelled. Max came running in and saw the room.

'Ahh!' he ran to the phone.
'Mr Spencer, yeah! Will you come as soon as possible, bye!' he screamed, Max ran to me, he picked me up and took me to the hospital.

I had woken up and the doctor said to me that I would be okay. So I went home that evening. When I got back I saw that Mr Spencer was there 'I have come to the conclusion that . . . a ghost is living in your house.'
'You're kidding?' Max said.
'I see it's trying to kill you,' he answered.

As those words came out of his mouth, I ran across the path and on to the road, just then a car came speeding along and it ran me over.

That night I died in hospital.

So here I am as a ghost! 'Boo!'

Charlotte Pennock (10)

The Ghost Story

As soon as I walked into my big old bedroom in my new house, I knew straight away that something was wrong, there was something strange about it.

The removal van was packed with all our furniture and we were now ready to hit the road at last.

All my children were really looking forward to seeing their new house and new bedroom. After an hour, I was unloading the van and I took a box of toys upstairs into the bedroom, when suddenly I heard a big loud bang! I turned around to see what it was . . . it was a small ghostly figure of a man floating across the room. I couldn't believe my eyes.

'Oh no! We have a ghost' I screamed. It is now twelve o'clock in the afternoon and my next door neighbour invited me around to her house. I told her about the ghost, then she told me a story about the man that lived there. She said that he'd died about twenty years ago, he was a recluse as well. He just kept himself to himself. I was shocked, I couldn't believe it. I had been living in a house with a ghost! So I think now he has died his spirit has stayed in the house.

Kellie Dowson (11)

Ghostly Thieves

Mr Jones had a very big shopping centre, and he was a very rich man.

He and his wife and child all lived in a big house. But there was something wrong about the shopping centre lift. His workers didn't realise there was something wrong with the lift, they thought it was perfectly normal and when he tried to tell them it was wrong, they just carried on working and ignored him.

When the workers had gone home, he walked around admiring his shopping centre and the lift would go down, stop for about five minutes, then do it again, about seven times.

Then the next morning, a few things had gone, just vanished. He didn't dare tell the customers in case they told everyone not to come there because it was haunted. He told one of his workers to stay all night in the lift and see what happens. He agreed but the next morning they found him dead. 'There is something wrong going on!' said Mr Jones.

'What should we do?' asked one of the workers.
'Call the police,' said Mr Jones.

He picked up the phone and dialled 999.
'Hello! Would you like ambulance, fire or police?
'Police please! he said.
'Liverpool Shopping Centre!' he said
'Bye!'

'They'll come soon' said Mr Jones.

The police walked in 'What's the matter!' said the police officer.

'It's the lift, it goes up and down mysteriously.' said Mr Jones.
'We'll point a camera in.'

Next morning, we all crowded into the Security Room and the camera picked up the shape of Mr Johnson, whom Mr Jones had killed to get the Shopping Centre.

Dylan Westwood (10)

The Spirit Of Oakfield School

It was a dark spooky Friday night in Frome. A teacher at Oakfield School had left her light brown fur coat in the staffroom. When she got home, she realised that she had left her coat at work so she drove back in her green MG, parked her car and headed for the ancient building.

As she entered the reception something smashed. It sounded as if it came from the hall. The teacher crept towards the hall doors very slowly and peeped through the transparent window. She heard a noise, so she hid behind the hall doors.

Suddenly she spotted a figure standing next to her. The figure tapped her on the shoulder and she turned round to see what it was, but all she saw was the headmaster's body floating down the corridor. She ran as fast as she could, not bothering to collect her coat. She got in her dark green car and drove back home.

On Monday morning the teacher didn't say anything to anybody. When she saw the headmaster, he grinned and walked off.

At the end of the day she went to the staffroom to get her coat and as soon as she opened the staffroom door she saw the headmaster and screamed. She grabbed her coat and ran. The ghost followed her to her car and then vanished.

When she got home, a cold chill ran up her spine. As she opened the kitchen door she saw a dark shadow gazing out of the window.

Antony Lockyer (10)

Ghost Story

It was a dark, dark night. The sky was moonless and it's blackness stretched out like the sea on the horizon.

A girl walked into a narrow, dark, alleyway. She had just come from a party. The party stopped at 1am. She was going home and the alleyway was the shortest route. As she walked, she could hear rats scuttering away and strange sounds. She quickened her paces. Then suddenly she saw her. A beautiful girl just appeared before her, she was so pale and so beautiful, it was scary. The girl from the party called Virginia stammered as she said 'Who are you? Where did you come from?'

The pale girl smiled and answered in a voice that sounded like an echo from a distant place. 'I am Adara, ghost of the unliving, and I've come to take you.'

Virginia just stood there, frozen in place by Adara's stare. Adara advanced towards her . . .

A loud scream pierced the silent night. It was over even before it began. The alleyway once again became a dark, quiet place. The only difference was a lifeless body of a girl whose eyes were as wide as saucers and staring as though she had seen a ghost. But she had seen Adara - ghost of the unliving, and the sad thing was that it was the last thing she ever saw!

Christa Korsah-Brown (13)

Mary, Mary Quite Contrary

Four friends on a school trip to the Tudor graves one sunny July day.
Eventually they reached their destination, but the weather was now wet and windy.

Upon entering the graveyard, darkness fell. Mary stopped in front of some graves.

'Mary I
1516 - 1558'

'Why so many tiny graves?' she wondered.

After lights out, they crept back to the graveyard with some vodka, Mary didn't drink any and they all teased her 'You're the Virgin Mary.'

In the lightning, the boys read Mary I grave.

'Mary, Mary quite contrary' they sang. The ground shook, Jody screamed. Out came hands, they had raised the dead!

Jody and Paul ran off, Nick and Mary were frozen with terror.

It was Mary I. She turned to Nick 'Thou hast stolen my babies!' Axe raised, she chopped off his head.

Mary ran to Paul and Jody, in the distance Jody could see Mary I behind Paul.

'Paul, run!'

Too late he was gone. 'Revenge!' she shouted. Jody and Mary were running frantically. Jody tripped and was helpless, three blows.

'Thou shalt go to Hell!' Mary ran to the door screaming 'let me in!'

The teachers opened the door.

'Mary I came out of her grave and now Jody, Nick and Paul are dead.'
'Practical joke probably, they'll turn up in the morning,' said Mrs Bell.

Mary sat on a gravestone. No one believed her.

Suddenly hands grabbed her, it was Mary I grave! She screamed but was dragged into the earthy grave.

To be continued . . .

Kathryn Elizabeth Callow (12)

Miracle Treasure

Once in 1942, there lived a girl called Nisa, 5 years old who was very poor. She lived in Pakistan and her family lived in an old house. There was a storeroom in the house where Nisa washed her family's clothes. One day she went inside and found a bald dwarf sitting in the corner of the room. He was facing the wall and when she touched him he disappeared! Then he reappeared, and to Nisa's surprise, the dwarf had red eyes!

The next day Nisa was playing outside with her brother Azam, (who was much paler and got ignored by the rest of the family) when she spotted a group of small children playing gleefully. Nisa greeted them and asked if she and her brother could play with her. They agreed and the children introduced themselves. One small child asked Azam if he could give her a piggyback, she *disappeared!*
Then she realised that they were children of a *Jin!

They always played from that day on and they grew up together. Nisa's best friend was called Qurechiaria and Azam's best friend was called Baranat. The other three were called Shamali, Mutapoliun and Khivaratna. But on Nisa's thirteenth birthday, the children were gone completely.

Nisa cried and cried. The next day Nisa woke up and found 5 rupees (Pakistani currency) under her pillow. She wondered where it came from, but didn't tell anyone. Then the next day she found 6 rupees under her pillow and every day after that it got one rupee higher. In three weeks Nisa had got 205 rupees. The next day her mum found her jar of money and asked Nisa where it all came from. She didn't say anything then her mum took a whip out and hit Nisa. Then Nisa told her mum and from that day the money stopped.

She asked where her brother Azam was. Her mum was shocked and asked her who told her about him. 'Azam was your elder brother but when you were born, he died after a day.' said her mum. She realised why everyone was ignoring him.

Straight away Nisa fell into a coma.
Who was sending her the money?
Why could she see her dead brother?
Who was the bald dwarf with red eyes?

Jin - half angel/half devil.

Mehek Mushtaq (12)

The Ghost Of Shallow Lake

It was 9 o'clock, Amanda was headed for a sleepover. She kissed her mum goodbye and set off out of the door with a backpack over her shoulder. Suddenly she stopped and took a piece of paper out of her pocket.

'Which way is Revello Drive?' She gave a shrug and strolled to the left.
'This isn't right!'
Nothing could be seen except fog.

'Oh I wish I could see through this fog.' Almost at her command the fog parted to reveal an abandoned building with smashed glass and opposite an old lake.

'I'd better turn back.' But the way she came in was now a dead end. She took a few steps back and felt something sharp. A sign said *Revello Drive* and it pointed to the left.

'But that's the way to that creepy old building.'
'Boom! Oh my, what was that?'
'It sounded like it was coming from inside. I'd better go and check it out.'

'Hello, is there anybody here?'
'Hello! Who's there?' squeaked Amanda.
'Oh forgive me for not introducing myself, I am Amealius Brown.'
'Where are you?'
'I'm right beside you, don't be afraid if you can't see me, then I'll appear for you.'

The wind passed through.

'Arrgghh! Oh my, I'm getting out of here.'
The doors slammed in her face,
'Don't worry, I'm just going to kill you!'

'No! Please!'

'But it's only fair as you are the reason why I am dead.'

And that was the last anyone ever saw of Amanda Brown.

Hannah Williams

Scream Dream!

'Goodnight everyone!' shouted Nina.

Nina had a twin sister called Nikki who looked and was exactly the same as her. Long black hair, brown eyes. They both loved scary stuff.

It was time for bed, but just before going to bed Nikki wished to go to a haunted hotel with Nina.

She didn't notice that she was rubbing a statue whilst she was making her wish. The statue was magic and it granted her wish.

'Goodnight Nina.'
'Goodnight Nikki.'

Just then, Nina and Nikki felt a shiver and then a force pulling them towards their bed.

'No one leaves the haunted hotel alive.' said a gloomy voice from behind Nina.
Then a booming voice roared from behind Nikki.

'H . . . how did we get here?' murmured Nina.
'I must be rubbing the statue which we had to take to the museum,' said Nikki.
'*Forget that! Run!*' screeched Nina.

There appeared a man carrying a dagger, about to swing into the wall.
Then Nikki and Nina came into a dark, damp room with cobwebs hanging from walls and skeletons hidden in the closets.

'*What?*' Squeaked Nina.
'Wait! What's that ? I feel something' said Nikki.

Suddenly there was a thump on the door. It was the man with the dagger.

'Oh no, it's a dead end, we're trapped.'
'I've got the statue.'

Nikki rubbed the statue and soon Nina and Nikki were in bed.

Neha Jain

Jack The Ripper

It was Hallowe'en and my parents had gone away for the weekend. My friends came round and we decided to go to the London Dungeons.

The trains got delayed and by then it was midnight. It was closed, we all gave a disappointed sigh. Then my friend said 'We've got this far, let's just go in.'
'No, we can't, it's wrong!' said another of my friends.
'Are you scared?' said my other friend.
'No!' my friend said in an annoyed way.
'Come on guys. Let's go in, there's an open door there!' I said pointing towards the door. We went inside and a ghost came floating towards us.
'I am Jack the Ripper.'
At those words I froze, I knew he was a murderer.
'Here to murder again!'
We all screamed.
He approached us and we ran for the door. But he blew it closed, it made a huge bang.

Just as Jack the Ripper got close to us a man came in and turned on the lights that lit up the Dungeon. When I looked around, Jack the Ripper was gone.

'Did you creep in?' said the man.
'No!' I lied 'we got locked in.'
'You must be terrified,' he said.
'No, we're fine!' I lied again 'we'll go.'

When I arrived home, it was 2.00am so I went straight to bed.

Shareen Hearn

The Ghost That Wanted To Play

Once upon a time in a far away land there was an old house, and in that house there was a little boy named Tom.

But Tom was not the same as all the other boys because he was scared of the dark, so every time he switched off the light he thought a ghost came in. Every night was the same and he could only go to sleep if the light was on in his room.

One night Tom was fast asleep in his bedroom, high up in the loft. He was dreaming about his scooter and didn't know that a real ghost had come into his room. The ghost had always wanted a scooter, and knew that Tom had one, so the ghost put Tom's scooter into a brown bag and disappeared from Tom's bedroom.

In the morning Tom looked and looked in his room, but he could not see his scooter anywhere. Suddenly he heard a bang so he looked out of his window and saw his scooter poking out of a brown paper bag. He dashed down the stairs to get his scooter, and then he saw the ghost trapped under the scooter, but he wasn't scared because he could see that the ghost was hurt and sad, so Tom moved his scooter and the ghost vanished.

After that Tom was never scared of the dark again and he left an old toy in the garden in case the ghost wanted to play again.

Aimee O'Reilly

The Black Knight

Dark night, dark world. A shadow moves, the Black Knight has emerged. He has battered armour which is dented and a night-black helmet. He has a sword smothered in bloodstains. A shield represents death (any limbs or skin?) Never! If you looked at him from a distance, you would scream.

Walking to Silver Castle in pure moonlight plotting to take over the world in one simple step. To take over Silver Castle, it is swarming with knights who are guarding it.

The Black Knight is at the castle. He thrusts the doors open. *Smash!* The Black Knight battles the guards. After a ferocious bloody battle a few seconds later the guards are sprawled on the filthy castle floor dead! The Black Knight slices his sword back in his scabbard and as soon as he does this, suddenly rising from nowhere, a Silver Knight appears from behind a cracked pillar. The Black Knight is weakened, but he will not give in.

The Silver Knight is a triumphant Silver. An eagle is embedded in his glossy shield. His armour is spotless and has no scratches on it. A helmet makes it impossible to see his identity. Good and Evil both slip their swords out. *Clash! Clash!* Both shields come up, then quicker than a human's eye can blink, the Silver Knight slashes his sword at his opponent's body, cutting through the armour of the Black Knight. His armour falls off - quickly the Good brings his sword down on the Evil and the sword goes straight through him. The Black Knight crumples on the floor . . . dead!

Daniel Monk

What?

We hunt ghosts!
Nikki, Kate, Nick and I.
I'm Jason, Kate's my dog.

In the summer we hunt ghosts. We sort of found one last summer.

I was reading an article in the newspaper 'Ghosts and ghouls at the Town Hall' it said. I jumped up and raced Kate to the door. I picked up the receiver '334655902' I whispered as I dialled.
'Hello-oh! ' said Nikki.
'My place, *now!* I said excitedly 'Bring Nick!'

'Read about the ghosts?' I asked Nick.
'I was waiting for you to ask.' He answered.
He *always* reads the tabloids.

When everyone was squashed round my table, Nick explained to Nikki.
'Let's camp at my place, we'll explore tonight.' exclaimed Nikki
'No you don't!' protested Mum.
But I sneaked round after pretending to go to bed.

Nikki's house is cool, it's green and silver with metallic transfers.
Nikki lives with her aunt you see.

Armed with a torch, a lead (for Kate), a hairpin (for picking locks) and sandwiches, we left for the hall. Kate growled constantly, a Brownie toadstool hit me, a bat got the sandwiches, but nothing else happened.

The next night was the same. The floorboards creaked even harder and cobwebs spun like candyfloss were everywhere.

'Let's go upstairs.' I said.

I opened the Brownie cupboard and went in. A child was there, eating sandwiches. A plastic bat lay next to her!

I closed the door and let her be.

Samantha Purvis

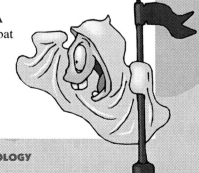

The Haunted Hamster At Hampton Court

In Hampton Court there is something people do not see that haunts the corridors, it is the haunted hamster! It's name is 'Hammy' and it was King Henry VIII's hamster. At night you will hear it squeaking on its wheel. This is its tale.

When Henry VIII was very young, he heard a squeaking noise at night. His parents decided to give him something to distract him from the noise so they gave him 'Hammy' the hamster. As Henry grew older so did the hamster. On the day that Henry died, Hammy escaped into the palace. He roamed the kitchens for food and was never hungry.

Henry's children, Edward, Mary and Elizabeth heard Hammy squeaking every night. They never told anybody, but they knew it was the hamster. Their children also heard the noise and were scared stiff. Eventually Hammy died, but his ghost still roamed the palace.

Every night he made a haunting, squeaking noise as though he were running on his wheel and could be heard splashing in the fountain of Fountain Court. In Clock Court a small hole was discovered near the clock. Whilst no one dared to say it aloud, they all thought it must be the hiding place of the ghost.

Every night at eleven o'clock, Hammy came out and played in the palace grounds. He stole sugar and chocolate from the kitchens and after a while people began to ask about the mystery of the ghost. The mystery still hangs over Hampton Court today and no one knows the truth.

But if you pay a visit to Hampton Court, do not be surprised if you hear a faint squeaking sound coming from the darkest corners of the palace. It's probably Hammy running on his wheel.

Tessa Tyler Todd (8)

The Evil Doll

One October on Hallowe'en, a girl Louise had friends round to watch scary films.

Louise's aunt and uncle sent her a doll but little did they know the doll was evil. Louise opened the present her aunt and uncle sent her.

'I'm going to kill you and your mum Louise,' the doll told Louise. Louise threw the doll in the bin, so the doll was determined to get Louise and her mum.

When Louise's friends went home and she went to bed, the doll got the sharpest knife in the kitchen and went to the stairs and began to say, 'One step, two steps, here I come, three steps, four steps, nearly there, five steps, six steps, almost there, seven steps, eight steps. Aha! Here I am to kill you!'

And the doll went into Louise's bedroom and said
'Hello Louise, I can get you now!'

When Louise's mum got home, the doll was on the stairs,
'I got your daughter and now I'm going to get you!'

Danielle Lilley (10)

Echo Of The Past

Beads of sweat were rising on Andrea's forehead. She tossed and turned in her nightmare. By now she was shivering in her fear. Andrea cried out into the lonely darkness. Suddenly, a ghostly whispering floated through the darkness towards her. It was so close by now she could feel its cold breath on the back of her hand. She felt a sharp pain in her back spreading through her spine, causing tears to well up in the corners of her eyes and then she woke. Her heart was pounding, she was damp all over.

The waking light of dawn was creeping through a crack in the curtains. Andrea slipped silently out of bed and tiptoed over to the door. Wrapping herself in her dressing gown she stepped out into the dim light of the landing. She padded down the stairs and into the kitchen. The tiles were cold on her feet and the boarded up window was letting in a slight draught. She sat down at the table to gather her thoughts. Could her dream be a premonition? Impossible she thought. But when she had the dream about her sister Jude breaking her arm, she did. It was like her brain was battling with her thoughts.

Ever since Derek had gone missing, her parents had not paid any attention to her and Jude. She was saved from her thoughts by the sharp, shrill ring of the phone. Andrea's hand was trembling as she picked up the receiver. Chilling quick breathing could be heard on the other end of the line.

'Hello,' she said.
'Hello Andy.' It was the first time she had been called that since Derek has disappeared.
'It's me, Derek'
'It's not,' Andrea said, 'You're dead!'
'I'm not dead, I live in a half world, I'm dead and alive!'

Silence.

'Andy, it's me. Please believe me!'

That was too much for Andrea, she opened her mouth, showing her sparkling white teeth and screamed. She heard the click of the receiver and then the line went dead.

That night (it was a full moon) Andrea was wandering casually up the street when she felt two icy cold hands grasping her shoulders and begin to lead her up to the courtyard of the church. Only when they reached it, did she turn . . .

Standing behind her was the transparent but distinct outline of a young boy of about 10 years old. The features of his face were indistinct. It was then that he held out his hand and there lying in his palm was the silver bangle which Derek always wore with his name engraved, lightly on it.

'Take it!' he said, 'Wear it always and remember me!'

Andrea retrieved it slowly from his grasp. Then slowly the thin blue line of his figure faded . . .

'Who are you?' Andrea asked.

'I told you,' he said, 'it's me Derek!'

Then as if a whirlpool had sucked him down, he simply melted down into his grave.

As the full moon rose a faint whispering ghostly voice drifted on the air,
'It's me Derek . . .' As if it was an echo of the past.

Pippa Tess Bailey (9)

Paint The Basement Green

Joe decided to paint his basement while all the family were out. He had his paintpots, his brushes and a flask of hot drink. It was time to start! Joe opened the first pot of paint and dipped his brush in and started painting.

It was a bright green, it looked great. Joe had been painting for about 15 minutes, when he noticed the paint was going down very quickly, but he had not put that much on the walls. What he didn't know was that he was not alone, there was somebody else in the basement, and it was eating the paint.

While he was painting, he heard a noise like water slopping about. When he turned around to see what was there, he was alone. Joe carried on painting, the paint carried on going down, the sloppy noise got louder and louder. Joe could not see anything.

It was now 4 o'clock and Joe's daughters were due home any minute. There was a loud scream, Joe turned quickly to see what was up. He got the fright of his life.

Joe's wife and children had been imprisoned in the basement by the green blob. Their heads were on the steps to the basement and the bodies were on the floor. Joe had no escape from the enormous green sloppy blob. What happened to him was a mystery.

The blob was angry because Joe had painted the basement green and he felt threatened by the green paint.

Emma Dibley

Ghost In The Grand House

Mid morning one day in 1963, my grandma and grandad had just finished painting the old kitchen in their newly acquired house red. Suddenly doors started slamming all round the house.

The slamming went on all day and all night. When the next day came my grandma and grandad decided to go and get more paint to repaint the room. But downstairs someone had already got some paint and had laid it out for them.

My grandma and grandad worked all day and finally finished. The slamming of doors stopped and everything went back to normal.

Grandma and Grandad have got a ghost in their house called Elena. Ghosts are not supposed to like red because it represents death to them. Elena is still comforting the house and it feels homely with her there. My mum said that when I was a baby Elena looked after me and my sister.

Many other unexplained things have happened over the years, but that's another story!

Katherine Cotterell (10)

The Shadow Of Death

Thunder and lightning cracked outside as Emily's mum went out. A neighbour was persuaded to keep an eye on Emily. The atmosphere went cold so Emily decided to go to bed. It was 11 o'clock.

Suddenly the lights went out. She got shivers down her spine and shuddered. She reached for the torch out of her bedside cabinet and shone the torch around her room and down the stairs. She could see no one.

Emily heard the gates clanking together outside. She looked through her curtained window, but still no one was there. Emily hopped back into bed. She heard a rustling sound downstairs. Emily clamped her eyes shut. Out of the darkness she heard footsteps and a deep, hollow voice said
'I'm on the first step Emily. I'm on the second step Emily . . . I'm on the third step Emily . . . I'm on the fourth step Emily . . . I'm on the fifth step Emily . . . I'm on the landing Emily.'

A huge black shadowy figure floated into her room. Emily screamed! At that moment, her mum came through the rusty old gate. As she looked up, she saw Emily's face at the window. Emily's mum ran inside and anxiously called her daughter. When she looked in Emily's bed, she found Emily's body but . . . her head was still on the window sill.

Sarah Beeby (10)

The Hotel Murder

One day my sister, mum and I went on holiday. We stayed in a really nice hotel. One morning we decided to go swimming. As we were walking down the stairs, the cleaners were then starting to clean the rooms. We made our way down to the sea. We stayed there for about an hour and a half, then we went back to the hotel to get changed and then something to eat.

We walked into our room and there were blood splashes all around the bed, there was blood dripping out of the wardrobe. We called the hotel manager and asked him what had happened. He just said that he didn't know anything about it and walked off in a hurry. We then called the police and they came to investigate. They opened the wardrobe door and the cleaner's body fell out, all covered in blood. They took her body away to find out how and when she died. The police took fingerprints off everyone that was staying at the hotel and all of the staff.

The police then matched the fingerprints of those in room 102, a couple of people were asked to go down to the station and take a statement. These people included the other cleaner, manager and the chef.

In the end, the manager and the chef were put in prison for murdering the cleaner, Jo.

Amy Pollington

Terrifying Brother

As always, I was being bullied by my terrifying brother, hitting, punching and slapping me.

My mum was having a right go at my brother for bullying me all the time, so I went to the library down the road, to see if any books were good to borrow.

I was particularly looking for scary stories as we were doing them at school.

I was looking down the aisle where all the books were about spooky ghosts. There was a sudden chill down my back, I looked around but no one was there but I saw the most frightful book ever. It was good because it was about haunting so that's OK for my brother, so I borrowed it.

When I arrived home, the book mysteriously opened on a spell, to cure bullying. I saw the spell and it was simple to say, but how does it work on my brother? I read it and you had to say it to his face, so I did. After that I fell asleep and started wondering what was going to happen.

As I woke up, I got ready for school and rushed to my brother's bedroom not remembering anything that happened last night.

I walked into the bedroom and my brother was dead, now haunted with a sign saying don't do that again.

Callie-Jo Hoover (11)

The Lighthouse Mystery

It was a gloomy night, the wind whistled through the trees.
The moon shone up high and the stormy weather was getting fiercer.
We just got off the ship when we realised that we had no money,
and nowhere to stay.

The only building nearby was a lighthouse.
We asked the man who answered the door if we could stay.
The man replied, 'Yes, we have a spare room and you can
pay for it by doing the cleaning.'

We were getting ready for bed when suddenly we heard a terrific bang upstairs. Adam and I rushed up the stairs to see what was the matter, but all we saw was a cat. Then I heard a door creaking and I shouted, 'Adam where are you?' All I heard was silence, my hair's stood on end, I was terrified.
I grabbed a piece of wood and went into the room. I swung the wood and hit the light, and there it was, standing there, my feet went numb. I turned and swung the wood again and again, but it was still standing there.
The Thing said, 'Get out of here quickly.' But it was too late, I was caught. I struggled to break free from the Thing, but it all happened too fast . . . I was now one of them.

The only thing I could do now was to get Adam out, so that at least he could be free, the lighthouse was now my tomb . . .

Tom Bodley (11)

Ruby Necklace

Friday, 6:45: I left my house not knowing what was in store for me that evening. On entering 13 Friday Lane, I shivered as I considered their address.

The six hundred year old house, draped in poison ivy, cracks down the brickwork and rats running around, was *not* a good sign. Whilst raining lightly, there was a rumble as a storm brewed. On arrival, I was welcomed in by Angela. She gave me a list of emergency phone numbers and left me to babysit Luke and Lilly.

The lights flickered prior to going out. I stood in the light of the fire. A slight shudder cracked pictures, they tumbled to the floor. A sudden chill came over me as the fire slowly burnt out. Doors banged continuously. I froze in fright. An old man appeared. I froze again in fright. Walking towards me he held out a shiny gold necklace with a ruby heart at the bottom. He gestured to me to put *it* round my neck. He walked right through me making me jump.

Suddenly I awoke. I must have been asleep. The lights were on, the pictures were up on the wall. Everything was peaceful. In front of the fire, Luke and Lilly sat playing. Nothing had ever happened. It had all been a dream. I stood up. I felt something cold hit my chest. I looked down. There was the shiny ruby necklace from my dream. It was a dream! Wasn't it?

Amy Tosh (11)

The House On The Hill

One dark and dreary night, Stephanie and her friend Amy cycled up to the old house her grandma used to live in. When they got to the house the door opened.

'There must be someone living here.' whispered Amy. There was a frightening smell when they walked in, like dead rats. They were roaming around the house when *smash*!
'What was that?' said Stephanie wearily.
'Ahhh!' screamed Amy.
'What?' shouted Stephanie.

'A-a-a-a-a rat.'

By the time Stephanie had turned around, Amy was halfway up the stairs, still screaming. Stephanie chased after her, getting cobwebs all over her face, which covered the stairs. As she wiped them off, she saw a red figure disappear into the door.
'Quick' shouted Stephanie.

They tiptoed down the hallway to the door. As they walked in they saw objects flying around the room. Then suddenly a book aimed at them, flew towards them.
'Who's there?' shouted Stephanie. There was a giggle coming from the corner. Then a little girl appeared. Then she disappeared through the wall laughing. Stephanie and Amy went looking for her. As they entered the next room, a vase flew at them.

Then she appeared again, still laughing. There was a rumble as we heard a noise on the landing. We ran out of the room towards the stairs. To our surprise, millions of marbles were scattered on the wooden floor.

'Aghhhh!' they both yelled as they fell down the stairs.

Stephanie looked up. Where was she?

Stephanie Lorraine Cressingham (10)

The Ghost Of Watlington Church

Two years ago Sally and I went camping. It was a dark and freezing night. The next thing we did changed our lives forever. We couldn't be bothered to set up our tent, we just carried on walking until we came to an old church. When we got inside, we saw big candles.
'I'm not staying in here all night' I whispered.
'It's too dark to go anywhere else' said Sally, so we were stuck there. We got our sleeping bags out and went to sleep. Later I woke up and decided to go for a quick walk. I didn't walk very far because it was so chilly. I was just metres away from the church when I heard a scream. I thought it might be Sally. I raced back to see if Sally was alright. When I reached down to get the matches, the floor was wet but the matches were dry. I lit a candle. When I looked at Sally, she was dead, lying in a pool of blood. I saw a note on my sleeping bag, it said,
'It you ever set foot in here again, it will be you dead, yours unfaithfully, the Ghost of Watlington Church.' I ran from the church and never went there again. I hope no one does what we did two years ago because you never know when the ghost will strike again!

Sophie Culley (9)

The Graveyard

As usual I was grounded, sitting at home bored stiff. Wondering what to do.
'I'm bored Mum!'
'Well if you want to do something go to the shop and get some milk.'
'OK Mum.'
'Here's 50p.'
'Thanks.'
'Be back soon!'
'Yep, bye!'
'Bye.'

I slammed the door behind me and ambled down the street. I forgot what I came out for, so I had a walk through the graveyard and came to a stack of headstones.
'They look fun!' I said to myself.

I slowly placed my foot on a stone and a big gust of wind whistled past me. An invisible man I guessed it was my imagination so I kept climbing.
'I've been out too long, I'm going home.'
Suddenly I tripped up, it was a ghost, I ran home as fast as lightning, somebody was following me.

I got in and thought what had happened, I was in my room when my alarm went off - I hadn't set it. I looked and in front of me was that ghost. He kept setting my alarm off! I called Mum but nothing happened. My alarm went off every minute.

I went under my cover but it floated over me, now I was scared stiff! Ahh! It was my alarm clock, it wouldn't stop and fled to the graveyard and buried my clock and ever since my
life's been way better.

Abigail Baxter-Hunt (10)

Ghost Story - Who's Out There?

I suddenly woke up to find myself in a wet ditch, surrounded by rustling leaves. Then I heard a voice in the near distance.

'Kim, Kim, are you alright? Wake up!' cried my brother Chris.

'Chris, is that you?' I replied.

'Yes of course it's me, who else would it be!'

Next thing I knew I was standing in front of a castle door. The door was very dusty and there were loads of cobwebs. The handle on the door was covered in blood. I screamed.

'Shut up' Chris said.

'You don't believe this stuff is real, do you? Obviously someone is trying to scare us! Come on, let's go and explore it.'

Soon enough we were through the door and staring into a room. I ran over to the coffin, that led in the corner on the right. I opened it up and a shiver ran down my spine. All I could see was a perfectly white skeleton holding a rose in one hand and a knife in the other. I quickly slammed down the lid and ran but something was stopping me from getting out. I struggled and I tried, then eventually succeeded. I quickly grabbed Chris and then ran as fast as we could. I then tripped over a gravestone. Me and Chris looked at each other. The gravestone read:

Helen and Martin Barn, you will never see the light of day again!

We both burst into tears, they were our mum and dad.

Kimberley Hurley (12)

The Spirit Of The Valley

It was cold, so cold. Darkness crept over the hills, sweeping the valley with icy fingers. Mournfully the wind howled through the rocks and snapped closed the shutters on every window. The stars in the sky flickered and died.

Villagers locked their doors and windows, every night. There was something that lurked in dark corners after sundown.

Two drunks were not yet home. Meandering down the alleyway, they were oblivious to the many eyes watching them from the shadows. One man lumbered away round a corner. His friend heard a chilling scream, then silence. Aware at last of the danger, he turned to flee, and came face to face with a nightmare. He died without a sound.

Pale moonlight illuminated the silent streets, then was dimmed. Dust swept over the two bodies.

In one tall house a ghostly light danced behind the windows. Those watching would have seen faces lit by wan light, twisted, cruel faces, or screaming faces, or the vision of Death with burning eyes.

Down in the cellar of the house was a web, a vast, sparkling spider web covering one wall. From it radiated evil that was unleashed every night into a slumbering village. Flickering and pallid, the ghostly light in the window became a vivid green glare.

Outside on the streets it was cold, so cold . . .

Lucy Jackson (11)

Hardlock House

One spooky night I decided to check out Hardlock House so I squeezed through the gates of the old, creepy house.

As I approached the door, I could see lots of cobwebs, just then the door burst open but little did I know what was ahead of me.

When the door opened I found myself in the hall and I saw rats running across the hall and pictures of ghostly relatives.

Then I saw my friends head with no body. So I started to back up, I heard something moving. I looked around but something grabbed me, I kicked it but I felt metal so it drew its axe and chopped my head off.

Now as a ghost I wished I listened to my mum when she said 'Nobody goes in and nobody comes out.'

Crystal Whittick (9)

Hardlock House

As we approached the dark, gloomy house. We saw the front, wooden door made from the strongest oak. The squeaky door opened all by itself. We saw the hallway. It was made out of hard, wooden, thick floorboards. The sunlight came in. We saw a shiny suit of armour, it was dancing. There were gloomy, dark, wooden stairs with cobwebs. We stopped and saw a black shadow. Spooky music started.

There was something fading in the darkness. It was just a black cat with staring, green eyes. We wondered where it had come from. Was it a ghost?

'No!'

We thought our mums had told us there was no such thing as a ghost. We were turning to the door, we were shocked with what we saw. We were absolutely terrified. We saw the ghost but we could only see the outline and the shadow coming towards us.

We ran to the creaky staircase after a second, we were in a blank room. We saw the sign 'Exit' on the door, we ran out the door. To our horror we were tucked up in bed.

'Was it real?'

Mairah Akhtar (8)

A Suspended Sentence

'Where's Jenny?'
'I don't know! Perhaps she's escaped! We don't have time!'

The group had gone to Julian's birthday party. There was no Julian there though. They found him stabbed in the great hall of his gigantic Tudor home. Standing over his body was a phantom, a thin trickle of blood oozing from its gaunt mouth.

Now they were racing through the castle, the ghost's voice following them, echoing endlessly. It was a cruel, high-pitched voice, full of evil. Then they saw it. In front of the hall was a skeleton, suspended by a long, thin rope from a lofty rafter, where the inky darkness was a spider's pearly palace.

The eyes though . . . the eyes were like two giant pools into which the best of thoughts were drowned by badness. They were hollow and lifeless but alive with horror, dissolving into whirlpools of despair and death. Its nose was a mere hole, decaying and putrid, apparently, sculpted into that flattened shape. The mouth was at an odd angle, a fixed crescent smile - gleeful, mocking, leering. Above the eye was a hairline crevice sweeping over the cheek. Adorning its cracked skull was a Tudor style hat, a large plum feather protruding from the green velvet.

The skeleton had not been there before - but how could it not have been? It was old. They knew who it was though, by the gold ring on its left finger. It was Jenny. And by midnight seven more had joined her.

James Hancock-Evans (10)

The Ghostly Atmosphere

'Creek' went the trees around me. As it was raining, thundering and windy. I wrapped up warmly as I knew it was going to be a long night.

'Hhh!' I was shocked to see and hear the bushes behind me start to hussle. Flash went the lightning.
'Ahh' I screamed as I saw shadows on the trees (of figures) I ran quickly through the wood as all I was to hear was crunchy leaves and snapping twigs.
'Thud' I had fallen over and surrounding me were lit up eyes in the holes of the trees.

'Ahh' I screamed once again as bats were fluttering around me. I crawled up and swung my arms around then ran. Behind me I could hear footsteps and because I kept turning my head, *bang*, I had knocked myself out - bashing into a tree.

I must have been asleep for hours because when I woke up, it was darker than when I got knocked out. It was a tight squeeze so I couldn't move and it smelt of mud.

I started to cry 'Help' but there was no answer.

I began to think about where I was. Then suddenly I thought mud - underground and black - coffin.
'Whoosh' I knew it, I was somewhere else. I opened my eyes and found I was in my room but I knew for sure, it wasn't a dream.

Sarah Thorley (12)

The Night Of Horror With Dadularr

Downstairs in the Young household, there were noises, lots of noises. Banging, smashing and crashing. These voices woke up Jack and Jill Young. As they woke they heard a scream. They decided to check it out so they crept downstairs to find out what mysterious creature or thing could be waiting their arrival.

When they got downstairs they searched in the dining room and the living room but the noises seemed to be coming from the kitchen. As they stepped in, they saw a shadow in the distance. It seemed to be looking at them, it was coming towards them, each time stepping closer and closer. He was approaching Jack and Jill in no rush but when he got to them, he turned on the light.

It was Dad!

Alex Cust (9)

The Castle

Clem, Jake and Lucy decided to go to the park. They were exploring when they came across a dark, smelly cave. They ran through it (because it was scary) and came across a castle. It was very old, and was crumbling in many places. Lucy ran forward, tripped over an old discarded brick and plummeted head first into a 100 foot pit. Lucy screamed until her frail body thudded at the bottom.

The shock of the fall killed Lucy, and her spirit rose out of her and floated back up the pit. Clem and Jake saw the spirit and ran for their lives down some stone steps near the entrance of the castle. The steps led down to the dark and damp dungeon, where Clem and Jake were now trapped. They could see other skeletons. They freaked out and started screaming. The spirit was floating towards them . . . If you were in the park that day, you would have heard the last screams of poor Clem and Jake.

Some people say their skeletons lie there today, whilst the spirit roams around the castle looking for people to murder.

Sarah Lamb (11)

Ghost's Night

I snuggled further down and pulled the duvet over my head. Now I wished I had never taken the dare. I once more recalled Cassie Harlow's smug face when she'd told me.

'Cathy' she'd smirked
'Your dare is to sleep at the haunted manor.'
I'm positive my eyebrows had shot up immediately. I had glared at Cassie before disappearing to collect a sleeping bag and duvet.

It was now gone midnight according to my glow-in-the-dark watch. Suddenly I heard an eerie noise. I shuddered and closed my eyes, desperately trying to shut out the horrific noise. I was terrified. The sound continued and kept getting closer, then I heard giggling. I leapt out of my sleeping bag and straightened my jeans and tank top, before running into the hall. I was fuming, as Cassie Harlow was stood there. 'Ooooohhhh!' she cried when she caught sight of me. She was bent over double with laughter. I marched towards her and glared into her eyes. I grabbed hold of her arm and raised my hand to slap her, when I glanced behind her, up the stairs and gasped. My hand dropped.

Cassie followed my gaze and stared. The most ghastly apparition was slowly flying down the great staircase. It was wearing tatty trousers and a T-shirt. In its hand it brandished a knife. The blade gleamed dangerously. I was completely paralysed. It continued to gain on us.

Suddenly I felt a blade on my neck and everything went red, then black.

Cathy Seddon (11)

The Haunted Doll

There I saw it, glowing in the distance, looking directly into my eyes, I walked up to it and picked it up. It was a solid gold doll!

I walked back home from the graveyard and held it out in front of me as I was walking. Every step I took was slow as I had to watch the doll because it looked weird. I got home at 11.30am and went in my house.

I laid it down on the window ledge and watched TV. My mum and dad were probably upstairs asleep. It was now my bedtime. I went upstairs.

I walked up the stairs and went to open my bedroom door, but the door was already open! I went inside and saw my pen knife missing. I got into bed and tried to forget about it then I thought, where is the doll? It wasn't on the window ledge. I then heard a voice:
'I'm in your mum and dad's room, I've got a knife, I'm near their hearts, they're dead!'

Then I head tiny footsteps and the same in my room, opened my eyes.

I saw clouds everywhere and my mum and dad. We were in Heaven! Then I felt a plonk.

I was on my bed again with my mum and dad. We were back! I heard: 'I've done you a favour.' The doll had brought us all back alive again.

Alexandra Caddy (11)

The Ghost In The Clock

The clock ticked. Tick-tock, tick-tock.

The wind whipped wildly outside, lashing the rattling windows. The darkness droned drearily and only the leaves danced alone. Everything was deserted, not one mouse crept, not one bird flew across the starless sky and not one person dared to step outside the warm comfort of their homes.

It seemed as if everybody, everything, knew what was waiting in the immoral town of Bauxdale.

But there was one, one innocent but foolish young boy, who decided to roam the cold streets. He took one step and there was a soft silence, which surged through the town gently. Suddenly, all he could hear was the ticking of the clock, the dark house through the woods. He was drawn closer, as if he was almost hypnotised by its superiority over his own common sense.

After running through the damp woods, he reached the house. The windows were all boarded up or broken and the paint had peeled off the door. He turned the rusty doorknob; it creaked. He pushed gently, and it opened almost too easily, like an unopened door. But there was nothing new about it, as it felt cold and used.

Inside it was freezing, but there was no way any breeze could even creep through.

The room was tedious, but the clock glowed invitingly. He felt its warmness as he drew closer and closer, it was starting to get hotter, he attained the clock and placed his frozen fingers on the once humid face of the clock.

He sighed relief, but then the face changed into a bitterly cold one. The boy's eyes widened as he saw the face transform into an evil, icy stare. The devilish grin chuckled evilly even though it did not speak.

The boy tried to run but with every struggle, the grip became stronger. Without warning he was sucked into the clock, never to see the light of day again.

He screamed for his parents, but all they heard was the daily news drowning out their beloved son's last desperate pleas for help.

Tejal Parmar (14)

Your Wish Might Just Come True

'I hate you!' You're a selfish mean girl!' said Jenny.
'Well I found it first!' replied Stephanie sourly,
Stephanie had found a two pound coin on the ground but Jenny said it was hers.
'I wish you would just . . . just disappear!' shouted Jenny.

The next day Stephanie wasn't at school. Oh no! Jenny was feeling guilty. When she got home she phoned Stephanie. Nobody answered. She's probably gone out somewhere thought Jenny. Meanwhile, Stephanie was wandering along the streets trying to think of an excuse for being off that day.
'Wow!' Standing in front of her was this really, scary, derelict house. Stephanie is really interested in spooky houses, so she decided to explore. The long winding stairs jumping out at her, the rattling chains and crumbling walls.

She loves that sort of thing, she climbed up the winding stairs, *Creeeaakkk*! Stephanie jumped back startled by the noise. After a while she carried on. Stephanie found a door saying 'Enter at your own risk!' Stephanie didn't see this so she entered the room. A pale, sad, young girl stood in the centre of the bleak room.

She seemed to be guarding a box,
'Save me!' she said,
'Um . . . can I help?' She asked as timid as a mouse.
'Do not come any closer or you will get hurt!'
The door shut with a bang and the lights went out.
'Ahh!' Stephanie screamed.
She was left in the dark with a ghost and no one ever saw her again.

Kimberley McTwan (11)

Ghost Story

I had a sleepless night that dark, December night . . . the creeper tapped incessantly on the scratched windowpane. The wind howled like a werewolf as it blundered round the house. I woke suddenly and sprang up like a mechanical doll. I do not know what woke me up, perhaps it was a bad dream. I peered around, staring into the darkness which enfolded me. My eyesight was of very little use. I could just make out the shadows looming on the walls. I smelt the damp of the rain pouring down in a deluge and the faint essence of the freshly changed pot pourri from the landing. The door creaked. Unwillingly, as if it was being forced. It opened slightly and hung in that position for a few moments. Then it opened as wide as a gaping mouth. I saw a ghostly white figure grope its way forward, hands outstretched. It proceeded with slow, melancholy footsteps. I felt a shiver run down my spine, like cold water chilling every vertebrae in my spine. 'Ahh!' I screamed and reached for my bedside lamp. I pressed the switch and 'Clunk', everything was bright again and the shadows were plunged into their hiding hole for the moment. I dared myself to look towards where the ghost had been. I saw my brother laughing hysterically, with the occasional snort. I chased him, caught him and then he was the one howling. Then, I heard a creak behind me!

Alexandra Caulfield

Gateway To Hell

'Mark! Mark!' Tommy hissed, 'Are you awake?'
'I am now,' he answered groggily.
'Do you want to go for a walk?' Tommy asked.
'What? Like, on our own?' Mark replied, shocked.
'Yes Mark!' Tommy said, exasperated.

They crept out of Tommy's house at 7 Smollet Road and out onto the cycle track. Their shoes crunched on the glass and stones as they padded across the bridge. The whole time as they shuffled up Silverton Avenue, an eerie silence followed them.
'Let's go to the castle,' Tommy whispered.
'No.'
'Scared?'
'No!' Mark repeated.
'Come on.' Mark shook his head.
'Right, I'm going.' And Tommy marched off.
'Wait! I hate your reverse psychology!'
'I, actually, admire it!' Tommy muttered huffily.

They started walking in silence again, when they realised there were footsteps behind them. They turned around simultaneously and saw darkened silhouettes against the gloomy sky. They gave off an atmosphere that would chill the marrow out of your bones. They sprinted down Castle Green Street, adrenaline rushing, they reached the castle. They looked back again and were shocked to find no one there. They kept jogging and began running up the stairs to the Governor's house.
'Let's go and wait over there,' Tommy suggested, pointing to an old oak door.
'OK.'

They walked over and opened the door.
'Come with me and live!' a loud voice boomed.
'Who are you?' Mark yelled.

'I am the Lord of the Underworld: Satan, Hades.' He replied scornfully.
'So are you to come with me and live?'
'No way!' Mark replied straight away.
'Umm . . .' Tommy hesitated. 'OK!' Tommy said, looking at his feet. He then looked directly into Mark's eyes and said, 'Any life is better than no life at all, isn't it?'

Caroline Marshall (11)

My Horror Story

The wind howled like a starved wolf crying for food. As I ran into the dark forest, I could hear the bats screeching and then I saw them coming for me. I ran and ran as fast as my legs could take me. Then I collapsed.

After a while, I woke up and found I was in a cellar. I stood up and looked around. I was scared out of my wits and didn't know what would happen next. Then the door opened and a figure appeared in the light and said in a weird voice, 'Come with me child and see the real world.'

I went with him up the creaking steps. As I went through the door, I blinked and then saw a horrible sight. Buildings were destroyed, people were working as slaves and there were dead bodies everywhere. The man who brought me here began to speak. 'This is the real world you live in, boy.' he muttered.

'But it can't be. I live in a peaceful place, a happy place. Please send me home.'

'Wait, watch this.'

Then suddenly, I saw my mum on the floor, screaming for help. The next minute was a shocking sight to see, my mum hanging from a tree by several fish hooks. 'Mum!' I shouted. I never got over that day, and probably never will.

About six years later, a similar thing occurred. My nan was looking after me after the incident. Then, in the condensation on the window, something wrote 'I'll get you!' Then my nan walked in and for some reason, she looked different. Her eyes were bloodshot. They looked as if they were getting bigger and bigger every second, then she collapsed. I ran up to her to see what had happened. She started to jump around as if someone was controlling her, then all of a sudden, her head turned 360° and these lumps in her chest started to appear, which looked like the Devil ripping through her chest. Then it went quiet. I threw myself on the floor to see what had happened. The Devil took her away.

Then I remembered a movie called The Candy Man. I went to the mirror in the hall and said, 'Candy Man, Candy Man, Candy Man, Candy Man, Candy Man.'
'But it didn't work then,' said the Devil. Then I was sucked into the mirror and never returned.

David Welton & Jonathan Williams

The Remains Of The Ghost

It was a gloomy day when a girl named Katie was walking down the school hall to go to the toilet. When she was in the toilet, she thought something was a bit suspicious. Then suddenly, she heard a voice speaking to her. It sounded like a ghost. It kept on saying her name, 'Katie, I know you're in there. Katie, I know you're in there.' Katie went out to see who it was, but then someone jumped out behind her. They chopped her into small squares and she was never seen again, except her shoes which walked round the school with nobody in them, and that's all that remains of her.

That's all. That's all.

Lisa-Marie Sweeney

The Slimy Creature!

One freezing cold night, two boys called Jamie and Ryan were having a blast at their Hallowe'en party. Suddenly there was a crash and half of the roof fell down. Jamie and Ryan were about to run out of the house to ring the police, when something stepped in front of them and blocked their way. A giant, slimy creature was there! Everybody at the party looked terrified. Nobody moved. They were so scared. They didn't know what it was or where it came from. When they got over there scary phase, they ran out of the back door and locked it. Soon the slimy creature found them, but he was crying! A little child tried to go up to it and see why it was upset, but the older people at the party stopped her. He started to speak, but in a different language. Surprisingly, he spoke in Italian. Anne, the teenager at the party, was the only one who understood this language. She told them all what it was saying. It said that it didn't mean to frighten them and that it only wanted to have a friend on Hallowe'en. That was the only day it was alive. The party began again, this time with the slimy creature there. The party ended at midnight when the slimy creature went back to where he came from. The next day at school, everybody was talking about the exciting Hallowe'en party and the slimy creature.

Philip Berners (8)

Hallowe'en Night

My favourite time of the year had finally come - Hallowe'en. I love seeing everyone getting dressed up and having a good time. I, my cousin Carly and our two friends, Patrick and Richard, for some really strange reason decided to go trick-or-treating this year!

It was 8:30pm and Carly and I were up in my bedroom getting changed into our costumes. She was a devil and I was a witch. We were all fourteen and I kept on thinking 'We're too old for this - but hey, it'll be a good laugh!'

We met up at Spook Villa Forest. It isn't really called that, but all the younger kids round the block call it that at Hallowe'en - weird? Our first house to approach was number 8. We knocked on the door and a short, plump lady came out. We all shouted, 'Trick or treat!' She grabbed a black bowler hat and handed us a handful of candy or a pound coin. I was dreading this next house - unlucky number 13. We approached the door very nervously, then knocked the big lion-faced door knocker. We waited for ten seconds and nobody answered. Carly and I just said, 'Come on,' and started our way up the path. Patrick knocked on the door again, only louder this time. The door burst open and a gust of wind blew through. We all jumped. I went to close the door, but they stopped me and said, 'Let's take a look around inside.' Since it was Hallowe'en night, we agreed to the stupid idea.

Inside, candles were the only light. The walls were green - dark green. The carpet was red - dark red - *blood red!* I quickly jumped out of the way, but yet again it was my imagination running wild. 'Look, there's a door,' shouted Richard. We scurried towards it. Patrick slowly opened it.

We stepped inside and the door slammed shut behind us. They all laughed - so did I, but beneath, I was really freaked out. We took a few steps down the hall, when suddenly I heard a scream. Probably just my imagination again. The high-pitched scream rang through my ears a second time. This time I was not the only one who heard it.

Carly and I started pleading, 'Let's get out of here, let's get out of here.' We got no response from the boys, when a creaking down the hall started getting closer and closer. This changed their minds. The screams were just my imagination - weren't they?

Lana Montgomery (13)

Dead Sleepy Hollow

I heard the knocking of the gravel as I approached a sign which said 'Dead Sleepy Hollow'. I had been driving all day and I guess I was pretty tired, so I went to the door - No 13! I looked down on the ground as I was standing at the door and found a newspaper lying there. It was old and faded and a bit damp, but I could still read the headline:- 'Old Butcher Knife Strikes Again.' It was dated 30th January 1978. I kept on standing there waiting for someone to answer. I thought there was probably no one there, but I kept waiting anyway as I was so tired and could have done with a good night's sleep. Suddenly the shutters banged open and I saw a young woman's face, but it quickly disappeared. I lifted the old brass knocker and banged it down twice. The young woman opened the door, her dark green eyes stared straight through me. She had tangled black hair and a very white, pasty face. Her black eyelashes fluttered at me as if signalling me to talk, so I explained to her that I wanted a room.

I stepped into the hallway and was led up the stairs. I noticed that many of the stairs creaked underneath the threadbare carpet. The young woman led me to a room closed with shutters and turned on a flickering oil lamp. When she left me, I was so tired, I flopped straight down onto the bed and it let out a loud groan. I decided maybe sleep wasn't the best option as the bed creaked with every small movement I made. The young woman appeared at the door. She was carrying a dusty mug and a cobwebby plate with a disgusting-looking biscuit on it. I had been really hungry, but as soon as I saw the biscuit I lost my appetite.

As I couldn't eat or sleep, I thought I may as well go for a walk. I creaked the door open and creaked downstairs, wondering how the young woman had got down the stairs without them creaking. As I approached the front door, I thought that perhaps I should tell the young woman I was going out. At that moment, she appeared at the lounge door and muttered coldly, 'Go for a walk, please go for a walk!' and practically pushed me out of the door.

As I was leaving, I picked up the newspaper that I had spotted on the way in. The moon was shining brightly, giving off just enough light for me to read it. It said that an old man, apparently a butcher who had died in a savage attack a few hundred years ago, comes back every twenty-two years and kills prey from No 13 Dead Sleepy Hollow. I shivered and tried not to read on, but curiosity got the better of me and I found, according to the paper, that a young woman called Anna Johnston had died in the Sleepy Hollow Woods near No 13. Underneath this shocking news was a picture of the same young woman I had just encountered. I felt the colour draining from my face as I dropped the paper. I walked on and heard another person behind me, someone with a distinctive limp hobbling behind me. I continued, faster and faster and then I broke into a run.

Someone jumped on me and dragged me onto the filthy ground. I felt something hack into my back, again and again. I heard a man laughing in the background. My head was ringing and spinning around and around. The laughing continued. If you're ever passing No 13 Dead Sleepy Hollow, you too can hear the laughing as I show you to your room. I am the new 'young woman.' I have replaced Anna Johnston.

Alexandra Pryce (12)

My Scary Story

I was on holiday with three of my friends, Stephen, Davie and Karen. We went to Hawaii for one week. We stayed in a hotel far away from everywhere, it was in the middle of nowhere. We stayed in a hotel called The Mozart. There was hardly anyone else staying.

We went to check in and the man at the desk wasn't there. I waited at the desk for about two minutes and then I rang the bell. He still didn't come. I said to my friends, 'Wait here until I come back, in case the receptionist returns.'

I went to look for the receptionist. I walked down the corridor and I heard a bang. It sounded like a gun, it was coming from room 13. I was scared but still I knocked on the door. No one answered, I knocked again and then I walked in. I saw the receptionist, he had a gun. He looked scary. He had long black hair and really pale skin. He was really tall and he was wearing all black. When he saw me, he jumped out of the window and ran away.

I was really shocked. I went back to my friends and told them what I'd seen. They wanted to go and see if they could find the man, but I didn't. I wouldn't care if I didn't see the man again. My friends went to look for the receptionist, but I stayed in my bedroom. I was in my room for about five minutes and someone knocked on my door. I didn't want to open it but I did, in case it was Stephen, Davie or Karen. But it wasn't, it was a woman.

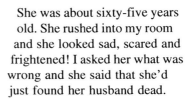

She was about sixty-five years old. She rushed into my room and she looked sad, scared and frightened! I asked her what was wrong and she said that she'd just found her husband dead.

She said it looked like he'd been shot. I told her what I'd seen and heard. She made me describe what he looked like. Then she went really pale. I said, 'What's wrong?'

Then she said that one hundred years ago, this building used to be a hospital. A man was taken into the hospital. He came back five years later and shot every person in the hospital. When he realised what he'd done, he shot himself. But now he comes back and any person who stays in the building, he kills. No one could stop him. He thinks it's

everyone's fault that he was put into hospital and he'd killed himself. There had been about five deaths this month.

I was so shocked, he had been a ghost. 'That's it, we're leaving.' My stuff was still in my bags, so I just picked them up and ran. I found my friends, I told them to meet me at the airport after they got their stuff. We went home and tried to forget about it.

A couple of days later, the woman's husband was in the paper saying he'd been shot and they hadn't found the culprit. I wanted to ring the police and say what I'd seen, but I didn't. I went into my bedroom. On my mirror, written in blood, were the words, *'I'll get you someday!'* My window was also lying wide open and there was blood all over my room.

Frankie Narayan (12)

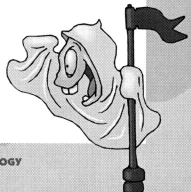

Catastrophe Corridor

While Sam was walking from her last class one cold Friday afternoon, to catch her bus, she realised she had forgotten her new scarf which had been knitted by her gran. 'I'll just walk on and get it tomorrow,' she thought, then it dawned on her . . . her gran was going to be at home. 'I must go back and get it or she'll think I don't like it,' once again she thought. Sam knew she had to go and get it, but it was in the other end of her school. If she went the long way, she would miss her bus, but that was the only way, except through the 'haunted corridor'. She decided on the corridor.

Neither Sam, nor anyone she knew of, had entered the corridor again since last year when the five students were brutally murdered in it. Sam was horrified - she had been with them and had been the only survivor. Sam ventured to the door, took a deep breath, assuring herself she would be fine, she pushed the door and walked in. It was dark and hollow, she felt a cool breeze brush past her, then she felt a severe pain in her side, exactly where she was stabbed.

'I'm sure it's just a flashback,' she assured herself out loud.

'Aaarrrgh!'

With that last scream, Sam ran to the door - she had to get out of there.

Frantic with panic, she ran to the door, pushing and kicking at it she realised it wouldn't budge. Getting more and more panicked by the moment, she heard footsteps growing closer. She turned to see who owned them, but there was no one there. She ran to the other door - it was locked too!

The footsteps were getting closer and closer, louder and louder, now there were voices sniggering and laughing at her - there was still no one there, then she got another shiver.

She screamed and screamed for help, but there was no reply. She continued to scream and scream for help, until she went blue in the face, still there came no reply.

Sam felt an incredible force pushing her to the window. She was being pushed by something, but not a human. She smashed through a pane and fell hurtling to the ground from four storeys high. As she fell, she glanced up and only then did she see the faces that had tormented her, only they weren't flesh, but sort of see-through. They were all pointing, sniggering and laughing at her.

Sam died with the force of hitting the ground. The corridor still lies desolate and is still a mystery. What did happen in the corridor that day with Sam? No one knows.

Jenny McKay (13)

The Night Before Hallowe'en

One night Helen was walking through the woods slowly with her friend, Sarah. It was dark and scary.

'Sarah do you hear that noise?' said Helen.
'Yes I can hear it, I think we'd better get out of here,' said Sarah.
'Aaaaggghh!' they both screamed because Scream jumped out of the bushes and chased them home. They locked the door and put the chain on but he smashed the window and jumped through.

'We'd better run in the kitchen and get a knife!' Helen grabbed a knife and stabbed him but he didn't die.
'Oh no, what are we going to do now?'
'I don't know, let's get out of here!'
'Maybe we should go to Karen's house!' said Sarah.
'Watch out, he's behind us,' said Helen.
'Oh no he's caught!' said Sarah.

They struggled and tried to break free but they couldn't. Scream took them back to the woods, he tied them to a tree with rope but they could not escape. Scream set the tree on fire and then Helen realised that she still had the knife so she cut the rope and they both ran away but he chased after them and then Sarah saw a cross lying on the road. She picked it up and showed him it and he melted.

Sarah and Helen just went home and pretended nothing happened.

Claire Emslie (11)

Ahhhh

I looked up at the dark, old house. One light was on in an upstairs window.

The wind blew harder and I was very cold. I went up the old steps and knocked on the door. The door creaked open, but nobody was there. I was frightened. Something touched my shoulders, I looked around, nobody was there. I ran up the dark stairs and headed for the light.

I rushed into the room, my heart was pounding. I looked around, nobody was there, then I saw it!

Oh no, how big, black and horrid it was! It's big eyes watching me. I could not move my feet, I could not escape.

I knew I was in trouble, it was going to get me,
'Oh no, here it comes!'
It made a dash across the floor towards me. Before I knew it, the spider had gone straight past me and out of the door.

Amy Gray (9)

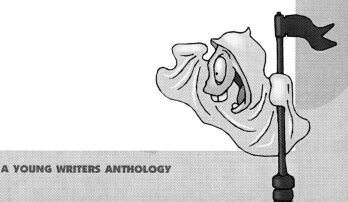

The House Of No Return!

It was a cold, grey, breezy night with every light on in the city. Then suddenly there was a power cut. A boy called Tom was all on his own in the house. When they fixed the blockage Tom found himself in a haunted house. Tom was a little boy with blue eyes, a small nose and thin lips. He had blond hair which was sticking up because he used lots of hair gel. He was very thin and smelt like roast dinner. He was wearing a yellow jumper, blue, worn out, denim jeans with light brown boots with the laces undone. Tom had a squeaky voice. The haunted house was made of dark, brown bricks and millions of broken windows.

There were about ten zillion skeletons on the floor. Tom was a bit scared. The doors were very creaky. There were hats, glasses and even gunge. Tom was very scared. There were cobwebs in every corner. Tom could hear a tap going drip, drip, drip. He could also hear bats flying and rats rustling. The house smelt of smoke.
'Hello' shouted Tom, 'is anyone there? Hello! Can you hear me?' Tom started to cry. Suddenly Tom heard the squeak of a door.
'Come here' said a creaky voice. Before the voice Tom could see a mouldy finger with big pale purple lumps. Tom went in and he saw . . . a ghost and a vampire!

'Ahhh!' Tom screamed with fear.
'It's alright, we're not going to hurt you' the vampire screeched. He and the ghost turned round.
'Mmmm he looks good enough to eat, but remember no foolishness . . . understand' the ghost said.
'Yey, yey, no foolishness, right, got it' agreed the vampire.
'Okay now, come on!'

Two seconds later . . .
'Little boy, what is your name?'
'Ttttooommm. Mr. Er Sir' Tom told the vampire.

'What a nice name, Tom, yes very nice. Now would you like a hot bath, Tom?'
'Ah, yes very much'
'Okay, here you are' said the vampire. 'But that's a cauldron' said a very frightened Tom.'
'Well, they just don't make baths like they used to, so get in there boy' the vampire and the ghost said as they surrounded Tom.
'No. I don't trust you!' shouted Tom and with that, he ran off to the old kitchen. The ghost almost got him but he disappeared. Actually he hadn't. He just got away but he wasn't looking where he was going and he jumped onto the vampire. Quickly he made his escape, but suddenly the ghost appeared in front of him. It was a dead end and Tom was captured! The vampire was there as well and gobbled him up. Tom turned into a ghost himself. He never did escape from . . .

'The house of no return!'

Zoe Charge (9)

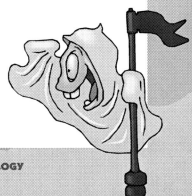

The Disappearing Man

Soon after midnight there was a noise and a very mysterious sound coming from upstairs. Then I picked up the phone and phoned my friends, I got a flash light and a knife and went upstairs. I heard it again. It sounded like a hammer being hit against a wall, suddenly I heard the doorbell ring.

It was Jamie and Luke, then we all went upstairs. We went to the first door and looked around, there was nothing in the first bedroom. We went to the second bedroom but still nothing. Then we went to the bathroom, there was something moving behind the shower curtain. I crept slowly towards the shower curtain and pulled it, there was nothing in there. The only place left was the loft. We looked into the loft, there was someone in there, he looked at us and vanished into thin air.

Then we ran downstairs, he was sitting in the chair, we crept into the kitchen and got the keys and crept to the front door. As soon as I put them into the lock, they burnt up into nothing and the door locked itself.

Then the floorboards gave way, we crawled out of the hole. We smashed the window and jumped out of the house. When we looked back, the house had vanished, in front of us, there was a ouija board.

It had spelt 'The Disappearing Man!'

Ben Sayer (9)

Beware!

While Daniel was walking Alex home on a cold and misty night, they noticed something in the upstairs window. The lights flickered and the curtains swished. They stopped walking and ran behind the nearest wall. They stared and froze as they watched, everything stopped for about 5 minutes, then started in a different room.

'Which room is it in now?' Daniel whispered.
'I think it is in the bathroom,' Alex said in a low voice.
The bathroom window steamed up and fiery orange eyes looked out. The boys picked up their courage and walked towards the open door of the house.

As they walked up the stairs, the house began to shake. Daniel slipped and made a loud noise. It came out of the bathroom, it stared at the boys . . . it was a doll.
'I remember that doll from the old doll shop' remarked Daniel. So the boys said in a bellowed voice,
'Let us take you to your leader.' The doll just stared and moved closer to Daniel and Alex.

Suddenly Alex had an idea.
'Run' he shouted. They ran with the doll chasing them all the way to the doll shop. When they reached the doll shop, they ran in but what the doll did not know is that when it went back in, it turned to normal so the boys went home and tidied up before Alex's mum got home.

Natasha Barnfield (10)

The Haunted House

One winter's evening, two girls, one called Jennifer and one called Claire, were invited to a Hallowe'en party.

On the way a storm began. By the time they got there, the thunder was crackling and the lightning was striking. They walked up the crooked step getting nearer and nearer to the big, old rusty doors. They knocked and the doors opened automatically. The two girls were squeezing each other's hands for dear life. As they entered, their breath was taken away by the gigantic, spooky house that stood in front of them.

All they could see around them were mirrors everywhere. When they looked in, they saw a big, black shadow. They yelped and screamed 'Aaahhhhh!'

Jennifer hesitated. 'I . . . I . . . want . . . to . . . get . . . out . . . of . . . here!'

The two girls were very scared. They walked on through the spooky mirrors when suddenly you heard a scream. It was Claire; she had fallen down a trap door.

Jennifer didn't know and she was getting really worried about Claire. Claire was shouting 'Help, somebody please help!'

Jennifer wondered where the noise was coming from, when she realised it was Claire's voice. She saw a tiny handle hidden away in the crooked floor so she pulled it so hard until it eventually opened. She saw a little finger down there. Jennifer ran away in search of a rope. She found one that was 25mm long and would just reach Claire.

Claire grabbed the rope; Jennifer was pulling so hard that she did manage to get Claire halfway up. There was no one Jennifer could ask for help because they were either ghosts or very weird!

Jennifer told Claire to try and pull herself up and after about 5 minutes Claire was up and running. When she was out, Claire spotted an open window.
'Come on Jennifer, this might be an escape route' said Claire quite hopefully. They crossed to the window and found that it was a way out.

The problem was, however, trying to get out without any of the weirdoes seeing them. Anyway they managed to escape down a very slippery drainpipe and ran like they had never run before. Their hearts were pounding but the main question on their minds was . . .
'Would they go to next year's party?'

Amy Andrews (9)

The Thing That Went Bang In The Night!

One Saturday night, I was buried under my duvet in bed when suddenly, I heard this loud, crash, bang, clang! I shook my head and went to turn my light on but I heard it again. This time it was a voice, a phantom voice. I felt dreadfully grim, it was like I was in a churchyard at the strike of 12.00pm.
'Oh no!' said a creepy voice,
'Charlotte dear,' shouted my mum,
'Yes . . . Mum!' I replied back in a frightful manner,
'Keep it down or you will wake Georgia up' bellowed my mum.

I got the kitchen knife from downstairs, I searched the house stabbing every trace of my steps. First the front room, then the other rooms as well but nothing in one single room.

The mystery still remains in the Robertson's house.

Charlotte Robertson (9)

The Haunted Swimming Pool

Gemma, Charleigh and Lisa all had the same hobby, it was swimming. They all go for a private lesson. After the lesson, they went back home. Charlotte just watched because she couldn't swim. The next day, Charlotte and Charleigh went swimming in a rubber dinghy. They started floating softly until a rough sway, then the dinghy tipped over and a red blood monster snatched Charlotte who then disappeared down under the floor tiles, Charleigh ran home straight away.

The next day Charleigh told the others and they went down to the swimming pool, about five minutes later, two red hands appeared from the drain. The lid of the drain lifted off and a red monster covered in blood, appeared with Charlotte under his arm. The blood monster ran over to the three girls, he grabbed them and dived into the pool into his dungeon, the girls all screamed but it wasn't loud enough.

With one bite, Charlotte's arm was gone. The blood monster had bitten her left arm off, all the girls were scared, then they discovered a crack in the wall, they stretched it so they could just about fit through, they managed to escape.

The strongest swimmer was Charleigh so she helped Charlotte because she only had one arm. When they got home, their parents were worried sick. Charlotte never got her arm back but at hospital, they did all they could for her. The four girls never returned to the haunted swimming pool ever again.

Lauren Agambar (9)

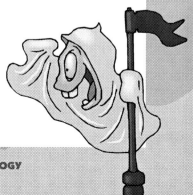

The Illusions

It was a day like any other day, I went to knock for my friend John. I buzzed on his door but no one was in, so I went to the back door, it was open so I went in and I scuttled towards John's bedroom. No one was in there, suddenly I heard a crash in the living room, I went in and . . .

There was nothing there, then I went in the hall. I heard a smash from the kitchen and I ran into the room, there was a cup in mid-air. Suddenly it dropped and then an illusion of a tall man holding a sword was there.

I ran for my life to the front door, it was locked and there was a figure of a man holding a sword. He threw his sword, it missed me and instead it hit the lock and the door flung open, I ran to my house and locked the door and snuggled into my bed.

Jake Skinner (10)

The Mystery

One cold and dark night, the clock struck 12. I was all of a sudden in my mum's new work place. I looked around the work place. I thought I better get off home but I thought I could look around a bit. When I went upstairs onto the second floor and looked down onto the bottom floor, I saw a massive demon! It was green and red.

I started running but as soon as I started running, I was on the floor, I screamed and got up and ran to the highest floor and looked down and saw stones in a big circle and rocks. I didn't want to fall down, anyway I wanted to get to the elevator before the demon would take me. I got in the elevator and pressed a button, then before I knew it, it had stopped, then I forgot that there was a broken elevator and I was in it.

I screamed. All mice and rats were scurrying up me, then I heard a bump on the top of the elevator and I broke the top bit and a vampire came in too. Then the vampire came and nearly bite off my neck but Buffy came and saved me and killed that vampire and that demon. All of a sudden, the elevator went whizzing down and me and Buffy got on top of the elevator and jumped into a hole. We were on the bottom floor, we ran down as fast as we could, vampires came out and started to attack but Buffy killed them off and we went outside and I saw my car and we jumped in and saw the vampires. They all came out and attacked us. Of course Buffy killed them all. Then we went off towards my house. I went to sleep in my cosy bed and Buffy went home. The next morning me and my mum had to go to her work place and when I got there, I didn't want to go in.
I said nervously
'No!' but my mum pushed me in and I saw a clean work place and it was all tidy, even all the floors were flashing with sparkle. It was a mystery.

Jessica Adams (9)

The Illusion

I came back from the playground, which was run by beastly dinner ladies at 1.05pm I came into the school and went to the toilets, they were very creepy, because every time I went to use them, the taps were always on; I tried to turn the taps off but everyone I turned off, came back on again. I turned to face the mirror and said to myself, 'That's odd.'

I came out and went back to the classroom, it felt cold and very eerie, in the classroom, there was a boy called Ben Sayers, he was a weird guy but I liked him. He was the fastest at his work, especially his maths. The problem was that when I looked at him, he did not always appear to be wearing the same clothes, one minute he was in his swimming costume, the next, he was in his pyjamas.

I was so scared, I ran to area 9, in running so fast, I smashed straight into a television set. Mrs Lynn was in the dinner hall giving a music lesson; I was so dizzy that I went into Miss Simeou's class. Miss Simeou came to the door and asked if I was OK, I did not reply. I was very shocked and ran out of the classroom into the hall. Mrs Lynn was standing in the hallway, her hair was sticking up like hedgehog's prickles and she appeared to be in a state of shock. Close by to Mrs Lynn was a strange figure without a face. The figure was grey all over, I remembered the school was haunted by a phantom figure, this must be the phantom.

The phantom said in a deep and creaky voice, 'I am just a vision, a scary spirit, a horrible, shocking, frightful, spooky ghost, a weird, grim, spectre or a poltergeist if you want to say that.'

The phantom then turned into Ben and said, 'Wow wicked,' but when Mrs Lynn looked up, it was gone. Then I looked up at the old battered clock hanging on the wall, the time showed 3.15pm.

What had happened to the time?

James Hackney (10)

The Missing Person

When they went in the old house, the clock had just struck midnight. It was getting spookier and cold. Then Jodie screamed, she saw something moving towards her and she screamed
'Aaaaaaaahhhhhh. Help. Aaaaaaah!'
Because it was a dead person and Josh said scarily,
'I think it is the person who went missing. His name is Oh'
Jodie said bravely,
'His name is Tim and he was . . .'
Then a ghost said,
'I am going to kill you if you don't get out.'

Then it went silent. It got up and said spookily,
'I want you Karen.'

Then a ghost said,
'You get one hour to get out.'
We ran to the door but it was locked and it had a spooky handle but we never saw it again.

Samantha Miller (9)

Untitled

In the distance, there was a spooky house and me and two friends went out for a walk and we came across an old building, it had all trees around it.

We walked up to it and one of my friends slowly pushed open the door, It creaked and there was a model of an Indian, it looked like it was staring at us but then we heard a voice, it said,
'Who are you, if you are trespassers, you are not welcome here.'

My other friend said,
'We are just looking, anyway where are you?'
'Right in front of you.'
'Arr' yelled all of us.
'Why are you scared?'
'Because you're a ghost.'
'OK bye then!'

We walked in the door, but there was nothing there at all. In front of us was a staircase, we walked up them. At the top we saw five shadows go past. It was ghosts and phantoms.
　　'Arrr' we got trapped and we fell down a hole that took us underground. A trap door slammed shut and we never got out again.

Spencer Eve (9)

The Hunger

She awoke with a knock on the door. Realising it was her boyfriend Robert, she jumped out of bed, feeling a deep hunger.

Her eyes were bloodshot and her skin pale, as her sharp fangs pierced Robert's neck. His blood stained her once white teeth, a deep, dark red.

Once, she had drained him completely, she felt satisfied. The moonlight cast shadows across the room as she looked around with her new found vision.

Everything seemed alive and vibrant, and all the corners of the room were lost in each other.

She felt no guilt, no emotion. All she felt was a strength that she had never felt before. Somehow, she had been given a new life. She was no longer herself, she was now a powerful creature of the night.

She was trying to remember how she had been given, what she felt was a powerful gift. She remembered the night before, the tall, dark figure by her window. The shadow that had kept her still with fear. The piercing of her neck and the screams. The screams that she had let out.

Then suddenly it dawned on her. All this power, this strength, this hunger and this urge for blood. She knew what it meant. She was no longer human, she was a bloodthirsty vampire.

Pietro James Catalano (10)

The Babysitter's Ghost

Once there was a girl called Jayne Smith, who was a babysitter and was once asked to babysit 5 babies for Mr and Mrs Keen from 7 till 11pm on Tuesday.

Tuesday came and Jayne went to Mr and Mrs Keen's house. When Mr and Mrs Keen left, Jayne's boyfriend Oliver Burton came round.

Jayne and Oliver were watching TV when the windows started to rattle and a strange creepy voice said,
'Lock the windows, lock the doors, go check on the babies, ha, ha, ha!'

This happened 5 times and each time it happened, something horrible happened to one of the babies. The first time the baby had been strangled, the second was hung on its mobile by a tie, the third had its head chopped off and its head was missing. The fourth has been stabbed with a kitchen knife and the fifth had been chopped up into ten pieces! By this time Jayne was having a nervous breakdown when Oliver went to the loo and there was a loud scream.

Oliver had been stabbed to death, Mr and Mrs Keen returned at that moment and Jayne was never seen again.

When Jayne's mum realised Jayne was missing, she called the police because she couldn't find the place where Jayne was baby-sitting and the police said the house had been knocked down over 50 years ago.

Some people say that late at night, you will find Jayne's ghost roaming the streets trying to get home.

Karen Evans (11)

Devil's Hall

A long time ago, there was a man who went to Devil's Hall and never came back. Now let me tell you the story. In 1853, this man went to visit Devil's Hall and people are saying he didn't come back because the Devil of Devil's Hall killed him by hanging him from his neck, then ripped his guts out for the Devil to eat because he had not had anything to eat for 20 years. Ever since he killed the last owner of the house. By now the Devil was dead but every time you go to visit the house, you hear screaming of the last person who was killed there and if you go in the cellar where the man was hung, they say you can sometimes hear the blood dripping from the man's mouth.

From this day on the Devil's Hall is now a camping site and when the moon is fat, you can still hear the blood curdling screams of the last victims of the Devil from the hall.

'Aaaaahhhh!'

Rachel Thompson (11)

The Executioner

Nancy never wanted to move. How it came about, I'll leave to your imagination. The point is Nancy, who'd lived in London for all ten years of her life, was moving to the country.

Let us pause for a minute and I'll describe Nancy. Brown hair tumbled over her shoulders in cascades of unruly curls, and like many people she didn't believe in ghosts.

Nancy shivered, she lay in a sleeping bag in her new house. She wasn't cold. She'd expected the country to be quiet, but it was almost as noisy as London! She remembered back to the legend her dad had told her. It went something like this . . .

In the spot where their new home now stood, an executioner had once lived. One day, the executioner was accused of a crime he did not commit, and was sentenced to death. Before he died, he swore if he was innocent and died, other people would be killed.

Of course Nancy didn't believe it . . . then.

She was just dozing off when she heard it. Footsteps. Slowly, her door creeeeaaaaked open, and there stood . . . a man. But he was . . . an executioner! He slowly bent over her and raised a glistening axe. Nancy was frozen with fear. Then . . .

The thud, thud, thud of footsteps. The creeeeaaak of her door. The axe came down . . . and this time Nancy didn't wake.

Leah Anne Eades (10)

The Orphan Ghost

One hot summer's day in Australia, Pat, Simian and I were walking the dusty road to our grandmother's house. This was a regular routine for us, we visited her every week.

The reason for this is that we are orphans. Our guardian, Mrs Dial, is okay, but very bossy! That's why we walk the three miles to see Granny every week (also because she is eighty-nine and stuck in a wheelchair. Don't tell anyone I told you though, please!) We must have been two third's of the way there when Granny's friend came hurrying down the road. We stopped her and asked what the matter was, for there were tears streaming down her face.

'I'm so worried about your grandmother' she cried, 'we haven't heard from her for the last three days and she normally gets me to bring in the milk.'
'Why yes, follow me.' So we followed her. She got the key and unlocked the door to Granny's house. Inside, all was quiet. Then, Pat heard unfamiliar sounds from upstairs. We left our escort behind and ascended into the darkness.

Then we came to the door of Granny's room. I opened the door and sudden flashes of light blinded us. There stood Granny, in a swirl of silver light and a burst of high, cackling laughter she vanished. I screamed as Pat fainted beside me. Granny was dead, a ghost. Pat's heart had stopped too.

Amy Innes (10)

Never Disturb A Ghost

Once upon a time there lived a boy called Cosmo. He was walking to school with his friends, Jay, James, Jodash and William, when they saw some construction workers were working on a house. They decided to go into the house, so they climbed up the ladder that led to the bedroom. The room was empty, then they heard a thumping on a sealed place where a door had been, they all ran to the window and quickly climbed down the ladder.

After school they went back up there, the door was still sealed shut, then they heard the thumping sound again, they tried to get out but the window slammed shut. A few weeks later the construction workers climbed through the window and found five skeletons, they saw the school uniform and saw the names Jay, Jodash, James, William and Cosmo.

Sarah James (9)

Recurrence

Slowly the door of the old Victorian mansion creaked open and there she stood in front of me, staring. I felt like running, but I couldn't, I was like a rabbit hypnotised in the glare of headlights.

Her eyes were pale and bloodshot, her face dead white, her lips ebony like coal, she carried an old Victorian knife. She began to float towards me, would I have time to run? Her greasy dark hair swung around her face, she wore no shoes, the white dress swept behind her.

This has to be a nightmare! But it seemed too real to be a nightmare. I tried to think of a realistic explanation . . . I'm going to die!

Run, got to run!

Bang! I slammed the door shut and rummaged about in my pocket, I had to find it. 'Got it!' I slipped my bike padlock on to the door and locked it, I pulled at the door to make sure it was tight shut.

The next day I returned with a *'Keep Out'* sign, as I reached the house, the door was wide open, the padlock lay on the floor.

I skirted around the house slowly keeping a lookout for any sign of her, nothing, I'd have to go back inside even though I didn't want to.

Once more inside the house my skin was prickling. Moving from room to room I came to the last room. The door of the old Victorian mansion creaked open and the she stood in front of me staring.

Stacey Dunn (12)

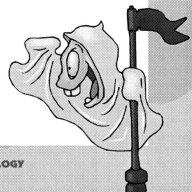

Hallowe'en Special

It was in the middle of nowhere in a far away field, as far away as America. The storm had started over an hour ago and got heavier every minute. The rain felt like daggers in him, coming from every direction, the pain was unbearable. It was suicidal just to stand there waiting for a passing car. He couldn't ring the police or anything because he would get a ticket for driving without a licence, he was only fourteen years old.

He had borrowed his dad's car without asking, to go to the party of Richard Smith to celebrate his return from Africa where he had lived for a year. But he lives too far away to walk in his best suit so he borrowed his dad's car (or you could say he stole it for the night).

'I knew I should have checked the petrol' he screamed to the emptiness of the stormy night.

It had been a good party and had lasted nearly all night, it was now 3.00 am.

Then across the road he saw a graveyard with a type of bike shed which looked dry and waterproof. He ran across the road towards it and never glanced behind him, for he would have seen the gate close behind him.

He didn't glance around at anything in the shelter but when he did he saw that there were many graves, but one of them drew his attention. *It was open!* Then he heard something behind him, he slowly turned and saw . . .

Kathleen Ingleby (13)

Cut!

Suddenly I turned around - a blood dripping werewolf was stood next to the dusty, old chair. Saliva was dripping from its yellow fangs. I screamed a high-pitched scream.

'Cut,' shouted the Director, 'take five.' Tom (dressed as the werewolf) pulled the warm, furry costume off.
'I'm going for a drink' he stammered, exhausted.

'OK, everyone you've had your break, places, camera, set, action!'

The werewolf made a fierce grab for me, I ducked. It caught me by the arm and started biting me. It felt real and very painful.

'Help,' I screamed, 'stop it Tom that's not in the script!'
'Cut, cut, cut,' shouted the Director, but the biting didn't stop! I was soon unconscious . . .

Claire Warren (12)

The Haunted House

Today Lucy, Sarah, Charlotte with Mum and Dad moved into an old Victorian house. Their friends told them it was haunted, but they never believed it. Once they were settled in bed, Sarah felt someone pulling her hair, she turned around and no one was there. She looked under the bed, and was scared. She heard noises coming from the window, ghostly noises. She tried to sleep but she couldn't. 'Sarah, it's nothing, it's all a dream,' she said to herself. She finally shut her eyes.

The next morning the girls went down for breakfast in the huge kitchen.
'Did anything pull your hair last night?' asked Sarah.
'No,' they said. 'Why, did something pull yours?'
'Yes.'

They had their breakfast and left the tall dark house, through the wide doors and off to school, their new school. They asked their friends, 'Would you like to come over tonight for a sleepover?'
'Yeah, sure,' they said. They all got home and settled into bed, and Sarah set up the camcorder. They fell asleep.

The next morning they looked at the video and nothing showed. Nothing happened for weeks. The girls decided to have their own room, that's when Sarah felt the pulling of her hair, and the mattress was jumping up and down. Sarah was terrified. She realised that things were only happening to her. She told her mum and dad and they told a sad story that she had had a twin sister who died at birth.

Jade Nugent (11)

The Ghost Hunter

One day there was a girl called Erica and a boy called Martin, they were brother and sister. When they got home from school they met a boy, his name was William. William told them both that he was a ghost, and the ghost hunter would come after him, that is if she saw him.

Erica was speechless; she ran out of the house and went to her friend Vanessa's house.

William asked Martin to tell his sister not to tell other people, if she did the ghost hunter would come after him.

Then the ghost hunter saw him, she ran after him and she caught him. Then she put William in a jar, when Martin and Erica got back he was gone.

They both said 'The ghost hunter.' They looked everywhere. The only place where they could think to look was the ghost hunter's laboratory. When the ghost hunter went out Martin and Erica went in and freed the entire ghosts in the laboratory.

When the ghost hunter got back she was sent to jail.

Vanessa Hodgson (10)

The Victorian Orphanage

In the city of Carlisle there is a haunted building, its eerie atmosphere and unkempt appearance makes it incredibly hostile. It stands on a hill surrounded by old oak trees and overgrown, neglected shrubs. The abandoned building used to be a Victorian orphanage. Rusty railings and empty gateposts surround the area.

My friend, Graeme, is fascinated by the haunted house. He enjoys reading scary books and watching horror films. Graeme begged me to go with him to this derelict building.

With torches we entered the building slowly, full of apprehension. The paintwork was peeling off the wall and cobwebs were everywhere. The dark corridors smelt of damp and rats urine. We would both hear the creaking floorboards under our feet and rats scurrying all around us.

As we cautiously ventured up the stairs we both saw a spectre floating down towards us. We were both incredibly frightened. The hairs on the back of my neck stood on end.

'Run!' shrieked Graeme. I didn't need to think twice, I just turned and ran as fast as my legs could carry me. I could hear Graeme's heavy breathing as he followed me down the dark corridor.

We ran home and told my mum everything that had happened that awful day.

'Dominic, what a wild imagination you have!' my mum moaned.

Dominic Skuratko (11)

The Blood Cut Finger

A girl was told she would be left alone while her mum and dad went out.

'Now don't answer the door or the phone' said Mum sternly.
'Aw but Mum.'
'No buts, I am going now so do not at any time answer the phone.'
'Blah, blah, blah' she murmured.

Bang! the door slammed shut. She watched as they went. 'Yes' she cried. She picked up the phone and was about to dial the number when she heard a strange voice. 'I am the blood cut finger, I am coming down your street.' She put down the phone quickly, her heart was beating fast. She tried dialling again thinking it was in her head, she heard it again.

'I am the blood cut finger, I am at your door.' She slammed down the phone and hid in her room. She heard the voice downstairs, 'I am the blood cut finger, I am coming up your stairs.' Thump! Thump! Thump! It was getting closer, oh dear there it was again. 'I am the blood cut finger, and I am coming in your room.' She held the covers even tighter over herself, it was loud this time. 'I am the blood cut finger, can I have a plaster?'

Jessica Young (10)

The Ghost Of Spooksville Castle

It was the 8th of March and class three were going on a school trip to Spooksville Castle. Clair, Sean and Carl were in group five; our team leader was Mr Pooch. As far as we know those three children weren't scared of anything.

Ten minutes later they were walking round the edge of the castle but Sean found this room. They all walked in when suddenly with a fright they fell down a trap tunnel which led them to a basement. Carl found an old white sheet; he put it over his head and pretended to be a ghost.

'Take it off, it'll have spiders and cobwebs in it' Clair said. Carl took it off and threw it in a heap on the floor and walked beside them. Clair and Sean looked behind them.
Sean said, 'I thought Clair told you to take that off.'
'I did' Carl said surprised.
Sean said, 'Well if you are here and so is Clair, well who is that?'
'Ahhhhh . . .' they all screamed and ran out the building.

The next day when they were at school they had to write a report about the school trip, Clair, Sean and Carl had a lot to say.

Jessica Lawson (11)

The Haunted House

One stormy day four people called Kyle, Sarah, Shaun and Louise had moved into a huge mansion. It was a lovely house and they were very excited but they didn't know that it was haunted!

When they were in bed that night they all woken up a strange noise, they all ran out of their bedrooms, the noise was coming from downstairs. Suddenly the house went very cold and they were all shivering and then they noticed someone had written on the wall, 'Welcome home Louise'! with blood. They all screamed.

So for the rest of the night they all slept in the same bedroom. In the morning they looked around a room and found some sand, in the sand there was some skeleton bones. At night the roof was caving in and Louise could see eyes on the wall and she could hear that someone wanted her so she ran out of the room. She saw an evil ghost and she stood up to it and a skeleton grabbed the ghost and tied it to the wall. She rescued the angels that cried for her and she became an angel. The others bought a new house but maybe that was haunted too!

Andrew Jamieson (10)

Death Cottage

One day Tom and Kate were walking down the path which led into the woods when they saw a rather old looking cottage. The sign on the door read, 'Death Cottage'. 'People are stupid calling a cottage a freaky name like that,' said Tom. But when they went inside they saw why the people called it 'Death Cottage'. There were old skeletons rotting away in the corner and bloodstains were covering the floor.

'Who's there?' said a moaning voice. Just then a dog came out of a door near what seemed to be the kitchen.
'Get away while you still can, the death dragon will be back soon' mumbled the dog.
'What do you mean?' asked Kate.
'Well the death dragon is a dragon who eats people alive, he needed a cottage hidden in the woods. The recent owners were killed by him and they now haunt the attic. To kill him you need to cast a spell on the house, but if the spell fails the two ghosts will haunt you for the rest of your lives.'
'We'll do it,' said Kate and Tom.

Kate, Tom and the dog ran outside. 'Say death three times,' panted the dog.
'OK,' said Tom. They said the words and there was a huge scream.
'The spell has worked' said the dog happily. Kate and Tom decided to keep the dog and they ran home in the hope that they hadn't missed tea.

Alex Rae (9)

The Forbidden Garden

The thunder rolled in the dark of the night. The rain threw itself at the windows in angry sheets, almost as if it was warning Marie to stay inside where it was safe, where it was warm. She couldn't, she had to know what was behind the ivy wall. She had to know if the rumours were true.

Quickly she dressed and stole silently out of the manor. It was 2 o'clock in the morning so no one could bother her, which was precisely what she wanted. As quietly as was humanly possible she ran down the gravel path that led to the mysterious garden. Being only sixteen she climbed over the ivy wall and stood in a place where no living human had stood for over one hundred years. All around her was silent. Slowly she ventured forward into the unknown wilderness. Behind her something followed, tracking her every move. Now she was at the end of the garden, the hairs on the back of her neck stood on end. More scared than she had ever been or was ever to be, she turned around.

They say she committed suicide, but no one really knows what happened. They say you can still see her, roaming the forbidden garden on a stormy night, but then no one really knows.

Amy Craddock (15)

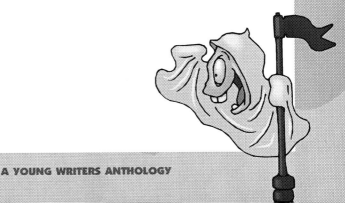

Friday The 13th

David's house, 13 Phantom Street was thought to be haunted. Everyone said it was but he didn't believe them. 'That's not true!' he would say.

Thursday 12th December - today's date thought David. Tomorrow is Friday 13th. He hated that day. Everyone said Friday 13th released the ghosts from David's basement to haunt him. His house was large, scary and dark and he hated staying in on his own. Him, his mum and dad live there in that huge, beastly, ghostly house. He hated it, always had. He went to sleep.

He woke up at 10.13am. Oh no he thought, Friday 13th. He got out of bed and quickly walked down the long, quiet staircase. He reached the bottom and passed the basement door. He looked at it, it was ajar! His heart raced. He slowly walked towards the basement. Down the stairs he crept, trying to turn back. He got to the bottom and looked around. 'I'm not scared' he thought. He took one step forward and down he fell. He looked up and saw his worst nightmare - Count Dracula! Then he ran straight into death! There was his coffin, Death standing beside it.

'Help! he yelled mournfully. He ran, ghosts following him, trying to kill him, swords, knives, axes, all coming his way. He ran. He saw a window. He dived out smashing the window and was instantly killed.

Followed by the ghosts they spookily said, 'Welcome to death!'

Cheryl Smith (12)

The Blood Bat

My worst nightmare is the summer holidays. Last year I was stuck in the countryside in the middle of nowhere (creepy!) This year we're at Bindstone Caves, I thought it would be fun, until I heard we were staying at Hill Street Hotel. 'Make yourself at home,' the receptionist said when we got there. I felt comfortable then, but when I saw my room I thought I'd rather be staying at Dracula's home! The curtains were torn, the pillows were as thin as sheets of paper, and worst of all the bare stone walls and floor were as cold as ice; so much for a well insulated room!

At night my dad ruffled my hair and said, 'See you in the morning Leanne, I hope.'
'Dad,' I laughed, and then I thought about it and realised he was right.

Next day after breakfast my brother and I decided to explore the caves. We wrapped up well and walked a bit till we came to the mouth of a cave. We ventured inside.
'Do you think anything lives in here?' I asked my brother, Max.
'Maybe some bats' he replied.
'Fruit bats I hope,' I said to myself.

We turned a corner and there it was with blood dripping fangs. We turned and ran, sprinting back through the cave, the bat hot on our heels, flapping its wings furiously. We darted out and threw ourselves onto the ground. That was a holiday I'll never forget!

Emma Humphries (9)

Three Girls And An Island

'Land ho,' Casey cried. She was standing at the front of the ship. A few loud voices were heard then out came Casey's best friends, Sheila and Mary from the cabin.

Minutes later the three girls had docked the cruise ship and were walking on the shore.
'Let's set up camp,' exclaimed Mary as she ran to a clear spot in the shade.

Once they had put up the tents they began scavenging for food and fresh water. An hour later they returned to the tent and snuggled into their sleeping bags. At about 12 o'clock Casey awoke with a shudder, she flicked on her torch and shone it around the tent, where was Mary? Casey fumbled for Sheila's arm and slapped it, Sheila gave a snort and opened one eye then the other.
'What?' she groaned.
Casey stammered, 'Wwwhere's Maaarry?'
'I don't know do I!' hissed Sheila getting a little stressed.
Casey thought for a while then said, 'Come on let's go and look for her.'

Five minutes later the two girls were dressed and out looking for Mary.
'Mary, Mary,' the girls cried, 'Mary where are you?'

Casey turned to face Sheila but as she turned she did not see Sheila, all she saw was thin air. All of a sudden a dark figure leapt from the shadows and . . . Casey awoke, in her bed, in her house safe and relieved.

Chelsea Lawrance (11)

Haunted Castle And The Vampire Aunt

Sarah had never stayed in her aunt's house before and she never wanted to for it was said it was haunted.

When she was invited she didn't know what to say, she couldn't say no but she didn't want to say yes. But her mum soon put an end to her decision making by saying she'd love to go.

Sarah arrived at Aunt Lucy's castle at 7.00pm and was shown to her room. The room was bare and had a cold feeling about it. Sarah was left to do as she pleased for one hour. She suddenly heard a creak and saw the drawer open by itself. She screamed so loudly that Aunt Lucy came up.
'What's wrong, dear?' Lucy asked.
'The drawer opened!' Sarah whispered.
'It's an old house.' And with that Lucy left.

Sarah sat on the bed, looking around, suddenly the window opened and a bat flew in. Sarah screamed again, Lucy came upstairs.
'This house is haunted,' Sarah said shakily.
'I see you found out our secret,' Lucy said, turning in to a vampire.
'Aahhhh!' Sarah screamed and then fainted. The next morning Sarah woke up wanting to suck blood.

Stephanie Pereira (12)

What Will Happen Next?

What was that? I sat bolt upright in my bed. I'd heard a bang on my bedroom door. *Bang!* There it was again. By now I was sweating and shaking all over. I stared into the darkness, waiting in case something horrible came into my bedroom, then the door slowly began to open. I was so scared I hid under the bed covers!

There was silence apart from the door creaking, I didn't dare take a peek at the door, but all of a sudden there was an almighty *crash!* Someone had come into my room and knocked something over. Sweat was covering me all over, my eyes began to blur because sweat was pouring down into my eyes. Frightened I took a peek out from the bed covers, I could make out a ghostly figure. Then slowly it began to disappear. I gaped at it in amazement, then I couldn't see the figure anymore. I lay shaking in my bed unable to move because I was shaking too much, I just lay there dreading to think what was going to happen next.

Sarah Anderson (11)

Haunted House

I was waiting outside the empty house for my friends to arrive. The house was supposed to be haunted, but we didn't believe it. I heard a noise from inside, so I entered through the broken kitchen windows, thinking my friend was already inside. I went through the kitchen and into the lounge, which was our usual meeting place. The only person in the lounge was a large man, hanging from a wooden beam on the ceiling.

The rope around his neck had cut into his flesh, and his eyes had turned up into his head. I wanted to run, but I couldn't move. Suddenly the man's eyes rolled in their sockets and looked straight into mine. His mouth that was open, formed an evil grin. The man started convulsing. The rope snapped and the body fell. It didn't crumple when it hit the floor, it landed on its feet. I ran.

As I ran I didn't dare look behind me. I didn't have to. I could hear his heavy boots pounding on the wooden floor as he came after me. When I reached the broken kitchen window I knew I didn't have time to climb out, so I just dived through. I landed at the feet of my friends who were just about to climb in. They turned and ran and I followed them when we heard the demented laughter from inside the house.

Vanessa Broadbent (11)

Search For Her Son

The fog curled around her ankles. The wind whistled, making a metal gate tap, giving the street an eerie feeling.

She scurried across the streets of the village, frantically searching for her lost son. Was he really here? All of the evidence had led her to the large house at the end of the street she was in.

The derelict village was old and dark. The only light hitting the village was from the moon.

She hurried down the street to find the dreaded house. Approaching the garden gate she pushed it open. The house was massive, old and falling to pieces. She dreaded to enter it.

Then suddenly a flash of lightning filled her mournful eyes and a horrific crash of thunder rang in her ears. She held her breath and opened the large wooden door of the house. There laid in front of her was a large hall with a flight of wooden stairs in the centre of it. There were a few doors leading off into small passages that had probably never been used for centuries.

She heard a slight bang on the ceiling and began to worry. She hurried up the stairs to where she thought it came from. She saw a glowing light behind a door. There she saw her son, alive. She threw herself at him and gave him a hug. She thought the nightmare was over, but it had only just begun.

Christopher Graham (13)

Clair's Spooky Experience

As Clair moved closer and closer she heard the clanging getting louder. The noise was coming from the next room. As she slowly pushed the door open wider the room looked as if it was spinning. Clair quickly closed the door and suddenly the wall moved back to reveal the way of a secret passage. Clair began to walk down the passage, the wall closed up again and it was pitch-black. Clair began to shake but carried on walking, thinking it was the way out. When she came to the end of the passage there was a door, she opened it and heard a particularly weird noise like hissing, the lights flicked on, it was hissing, all the shelves were covered in snakes. Clair screamed but nothing happened. The snakes never moved until Clair started backing away, they started to move closer to her and spit venom. She found if she moved back the snakes moved forward and if she moved forward the snakes continued to move back. So she carried on into the next room, there she found a key hanging from the ceiling but couldn't reach it. She looked around and in the corner of the gloomy, dark room she found two crates, stacked them and grabbed the key, opened the next door and found herself back in the forest. As she looked round the haunted house disappeared and she ran quickly home.

Sharon Royle (13)

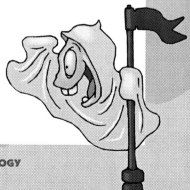

Terror Cottage

I walked down the back garden path. I was with two mates. We were walking around the new estate. We went to the woods nearby. There were no sounds apart from the trees rustling, the wind blowing and the leaves crunching. As we walked further on in the fog I could just see something in the distance. It was a big old cottage.

The windows were overgrown with ivy leaves, the door was tall and wooden with a glass window in front of it. The roof had wooden sticks on it with straw. When we walked up the path it looked like an old man who was disfigured banging on the door window loudly. When I banged back on the door, children came to all of the windows. These children looked like spirits.

I took a few steps backwards because this place beneath the undergrowth was weird. I managed to free the people from the huge cottage. When I moved the ivy there was a child with no head. I fell backwards. When all of the spirits floated off into the foggy, misty air, me and my mates entered the cottage.

There were cobwebs all over the place. As we took the first step up the staircase it creaked. All the way up them they never stopped creaking. When we got to the top we looked around the house and there were cobwebs everywhere. There was a spider the size of my hand. Then there was something ugly in the cobwebs that dropped.

Sean Andrews (13)

Ghost Stories

Me and my friends sat watching TV bored out of our brains. I said, 'Why don't we go to that castle down south?'
We all agreed so that day we set off.

When we arrived, the castle was so big. There was a man standing outside begging for money. We just walked past him and he said, 'Don't go in!'

We just ignored him. We walked around the castle, it was dark and gloomy. Shivers ran down our backs. There were steps leading to the very top of the castle but a door stood in our way.

When we were standing at the door Michael said, 'Listen you can hear somebody crying.'

It was true. We turned the handle of the door, but nobody was there, the room was a small and damp room. Then a little girl appeared. She looked about five years old. The tramp who sat outside came banging in and he said, 'I told you not to go in.' He took a small photo out of his pocket and said, 'This is the girl her mum abandoned her but she wanted her mum so much that she jumped out of the window. Now her soul lives on in this room.'

Some kind of magic powers lifted me up. I was now hanging on to the window ledge. I had to let go I was falling, falling, falling. Now I'm like her *dead!*

My friends tried to run but they couldn't! Michael was able to run but he too fell out of the window. Was this the end of the world?

Glen Middleton (12)

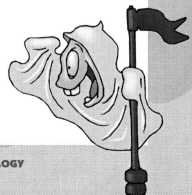

The Story Of Geoffrey Cook!

About 300 years ago, there was a 97 year old man called Geoffrey Cook, he was very famous and rich. Geoffrey lived in a castle in London. This was a very big castle and it was very old. When you were on the bottom floor you could go outside and there was a square of paving stones (that was never used for anything). On the 24th December 1701, Geoffrey Cook fell ill, he was rushed to hospital straight away. About three months later he was allowed to go home as he had said that's where he wanted to die.

His illness went on for the rest of the year, until New Year's Eve 1702 when Geoffrey passed away after he had sat down to get his tea and had an argument with his sister Mary and had a heart attack.

Geoffrey was buried in the back garden of the castle next to his wife's grave, then because Geoffrey was so famous, with some of his money his sister had a gold statue of Geoffrey made in the square at the bottom of the castle. She felt guilty about the way he died. This statue never looked like a normal statue and every New Year's Eve after that his statue used to disappear and people used to see his ghost walking around the grounds of the castle saying, 'You killed me, Mary. I will haunt you until the day you die.' This still happens now after 300 years.

Caroline Blackwood-Wallace (12)

The Hitchhiker Ghost

One misty night at midnight about fifty years ago, a young girl was on her way home from a party when something horrific happened!

She tried to hitchhike her way home. She tried her best to persuade people to give her a lift, nobody would.

Eventually a man offered to give her a lift, she accepted. The driver drove through a wood and he said, 'It's only a short cut.' She didn't believe him. She tried to get out! She couldn't.

The wood was dense and eerie. A man walking past heard her scream but didn't go in. The man murdered her in cold blood.

After the teenage girl had been murdered, she was seen entering her house. Her mam thought she was acting pretty normal but her dad didn't seem to think so. She went to bed, but when her mam went to wake her up she had disappeared.

Her mam came running downstairs and saw that her daughter had been murdered, it was all over the news.

One eerie night a man called Thomas was driving past the wood where the girl was murdered. All of a sudden something terrible happened. His car had turned over but how could it have happened because the road was clear.

Ever since, men that have passed the wood have been injured by the teenage girl, who was brutally murdered. She has also been seen by people. They say that she's been trying to hitchhike but when they pulled up she disappeared.

Zoe Hutchinson (12)

The Boyfriend

About 200 years ago there was a girl who lived in this castle with her father. She had a boyfriend that she used to meet every night. She didn't think her father knew but he did. Her father didn't like him and wanted something done about it.

He sat and pondered about it for two whole weeks. Every night his daughter, Helen, would go and see her beloved James, while he sat thinking. He thought about killing him, giving him money to move away and lots of other things.

The man's daughter never thought that her father, John, would find out, and if he did she didn't think he'd be mad.

Helen did not have a mother as she had died when Helen was only young and therefore only lived with her father.

One night, after a long thought, John got his dog, that he had not let eat for two weeks and took it out. His daughter was already out and he got a piece of his daughter's boyfriend's clothing and gave the dog it to smell. The dog started running and ran into the forest. John was way behind.

Earlier the dog had been told to kill the person wearing it, as John had expected James to be wearing it.

Now when John had caught up with his dog, the dog had killed someone and that someone was his daughter!

Helen now haunts that wood.

Laura Fannan (12)

The Haunted Hotel

After attending a late service at church, Rachel decided to go to her room. With her friend Sara who she had attended church with, she went up to her room, the room she lived in.

She watched television for a bit before dropping off to sleep. She woke up in the early hours of the morning about half-past three. The room had become bleak following this, a smouldering figure appeared at the doorway, it was Sara. She sat on a chair near the window, that blew dusty curtains over Sara, whose silhouette was now covering Rachel's face. She started to talk to Rachel, telling her about all the things that she wanted to do with her life. Rachel was only half awake, she didn't think that this was strange at all.

After an hour of talking she hovered away, her nightdress trailing behind. Rachel fell asleep. At six o'clock she was awoken by the wind blowing through the open window. As she sat up and looked at the chair Sara had sat on, she found a pool of blood on the floor dripping off the chair onto the floor, proving that it wasn't a dream. She screamed, but nothing came out. Moments after, the phone rang it was the vicar. He said that Sara had died last night at half-past twelve after falling off her balcony and landing in an unused skip. Unfortunately a piece of glass had punctured her heart and she died from loss of blood.

Jennifer Ash (12)

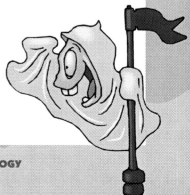

Dead Man's Den

Last night I camped out at Dead Man's Den with my friends Josh and Ste but the strange thing is I was the only one that came back!

It all started last night, we had just set up the tent when it got really cold and shivers went down our backs so Ste said, 'I will go and get some wood to make a fire!' So he set off.

About half an hour later we started to get worried so me and Josh got our flashlights because it was dark and set off.

In about two hours we realised we were lost. 'I know,' I thought, 'I'll use my mobile phone!' Then I realised my battery was flat.

Suddenly a big Rottweiler jumped out of the bushes and chased me and Josh so we both split up and ran for our lives.

I ran and ran until I was exhausted. So I sat down on a log to catch my breath, when a headless chicken came running at me clucking and then it disappeared. Straight after that it went cold and quiet but then Josh and Ste came running at me with knives screaming, 'You killed us!' I climbed up a tree but then suddenly they burst out laughing and I realised they were just joking.

I clambered down when suddenly a loud cry made me shiver. Then I saw Josh and Ste get lifted up and they flew up in the air and I never saw them again.

Lee Collinson (12)

A Mother's Vision

On Christmas Eve 1969 in London, a party was happening.

Thirty-seven year old Kaye James was hosting her annual party. Her two year old son Jacob and her five year old daughter Mary-Kate were asleep upstairs. Kaye was expecting her third child. There was a lot of noise with music and talking and Kaye was getting threatening phone calls about the noise from her neighbours. One phone call scared Kaye so much that she turned the music off and asked everyone to leave.

Later that night she heard a smash, then a whimper and finally a bullet shot. She ran to Jacob's and Mary's room. Blood was covering the wall around Jacob's bed. Kaye screamed in horror! She called 999 and asked for the police and the emergency ambulance.

When the emergency services arrived they confirmed Jacob's death. The next day it was all over the news. 'Two year old Jacob: Murdered in his own bedroom!'

Ten years passed slowly. It was Christmas Eve again. Kaye was downstairs wrapping gifts for Mary-Kate and Tammie.

She heard crying upstairs. She looked to the top of the stairs. A boy about thirteen was sitting crying to himself. He looked up at Kaye. She recognised him. It was Jacob!

He said, 'Leave me be, get on with your life!'
She listened to him, violently shaking, she replied quietly, 'I cannot let you go, you're my son!'
'You have other children to care for!'

Kaye realised Jacob was saying goodbye and let him go.

Lauren Arnison (12)

Death On The Moulin Rouge

The year was 1945, the year that Lou Cabalonie - a gangster - died. It was a fight to the death with Lou and Jerry Bega. Jerry had Lou cornered on top of the Moulin Rouge Café. The only way to save himself was to jump off the roof and hopefully land in the open-roof car below. Sadly he landed on the sidewalk. Jerry saw Lou stand up and start to walk away unharmed.

'Stop right there,' shouted Jerry holding his gun towards Lou. 'I will get rid of you,' he shouted abusively.

Lou turned round and shot his gun, the bullet hit Jerry, Jerry hit the ground . . . dead!

Forty-seven years later Erik Bega was twelve. Erik's great-grandad was Jerry Bega. Erik decided to cut through the cemetery one night on the way home from a party. Suddenly a ghost started to chase him with a gun.

Erik ran into the old Moulin Rouge Café but what he didn't know was that it was full of ghosts.

'Erik!' said one ghost, as he walked in. 'I'm your great-granddad Jerry.' Erik recognised him from photos. Erik told him everything he's seen and Jerry said he'd go and have a look at this ghost.

Jerry walked into the cemetery and there stood Lou pointing his gun towards Jerry. The gun wasn't a normal gun, it was one that killed ghosts. Jerry pulled out his gun . . . it was another fight to the death. Lou shot his gun but Jerry dodged. Jerry shot his gun and Lou was dead again!

Lauren Sutherns (12)

The Awakening Of The Dead

It was a pleasant day at Sunny Ville where barrages are set up everywhere. A new family was moving unaware of the dangers of the night.

They got to their new house. It was barricaded and reinforced with steel and cement. They pulled away the cages round the windows and the weapons.

Night came and after hours of work the family could hear moaning, gunshots and people screaming. Then the barrages across the street crumbled as the creatures of the night came from the dark night.

Some were crawling and some were walking but they all were moaning.

Their father saw the kids looking out of the window. He rushed down to the window and to his disbelief he saw the walking dead but he thought it was drunken hooligans. If he'd only seen what the kids had.

He went out leaving the door open, saying, 'Scram, shoo and get away!' It was too late the flesh-eating monsters got behind him and went into the house and closed the door.

By the time the father found out it was too late, they ripped him apart and began to feast on his flesh.

The same fate was to happen to the family but there was no blood. The family must still be in the house. It is said on the night you can smell the family corpses and hear the squelching of the flesh being ripped from them.

Stephen Dickerson (13)

Insomnia Or Death?

A researcher put an advertisement in the local newspaper asking for people suffering from insomnia. He wanted people to come forward so that he could take them to a house that was rumoured to be haunted. He did this to see the reaction of how they slept.

Six people came forward, Claire Wills, Zoe Carter, Sarah Leigh Smith, Craig Cromwell, Steven Jones and Adam Pounder. They were sent a taxi to take them to Hill Top House on Tuesday 10th July 1987. They were staying till Friday 13th July at midnight.

On the morning of Tuesday 10th the six people met in the ballroom of the house. Straight away Zoe, a well-known clairvoyant sensed the feeling of coldness. Zoe didn't like this feeling, she knew something was wrong.

Suddenly there was a cool breeze and all the doors in the house blew open. Sarah thought that she saw a little girl at the top of the stairs but when Sarah called for her she vanished.

Zoe decided to research the history of the house. Zoe found out that a man brutally killed a five year old girl. The people who lived near him thought that he deserved to die, so they brutally killed him. It was rumoured that the man haunts his house and kills whoever enters.

The next day Craig was found hanging from the ceiling in his room. They just thought that he had had enough. Later that night Sarah thought she heard a voice, so she went upstairs to see who it was. When she opened the door she saw a flash and fell to the ground. When the others went upstairs they found her on the floor covered in blood. She was dead.

Zoe said, 'There's something going on here. Let's leave while we're alive.'

They all got their clothes together and went downstairs. They went to the door but couldn't get out because all the doors and windows were locked.

Thirty years later a couple were moving into the same house when they saw the bones of seven people.

Danielle Miller (12)

Who's That?

It was a cold winter's night and I was driving home. The road was never-ending, it felt as if it was going on forever.

I had been to my auntie's house and had had a great time. I had been driving for ages and I was getting very tired so I decided to stop at a motel I passed. The motel was a small cottage type and very eerie.

Out from my window was a graveyard. I could see a couple arguing but it was about 2.30 in the morning. I couldn't sleep thinking about that stranded couple.

I went to go in my car the next morning and the girl was sitting on a gravestone crying. I went to see if she was alright, she said her boyfriend had left her and she didn't have a way to get home. I offered her a lift and had to leave her in town at a bus station. I gave her my coat so she wouldn't freeze and asked for her phone number so I could check if she got home. She agreed and gave me her name - Becky - and her number.

I phoned her later on that day and a man answered. I said, 'Hello, is Becky there?'

He said, 'No, I'm sorry, she died five years ago today.'

I said, 'She can't have, I gave her a lift to the bus station early on today.

He asked me to describe her, so I did. I said she had long blonde hair and a small face and she was wearing a pink top and black trousers.

He said, 'But that's what she was wearing on the night she died!'

After this phone call I was quite shocked, so I decided to go back to the graveyard and when I got there, my jacket was on Rebecca Colinsup's grave with a note saying, 'Thanks for your help!'

Laura Preston (13)

Full Moon Scare

On a dark and gloomy night, there was a boy called Peter, who in the morning was going to a sports trial for running. Peter lived in a very small and cramped house, along with his very nasty sisters and his mother.

That same night Peter went out for a walk and saw some very strange people walking past him. Peter was walking down the street. When he turned the corner, he saw the two people again. He thought to himself, 'If those two went past me, how could they have got round the corner without me seeing them?'

He carried on walking when he heard three screams, coming from the cemetery. They were loud, then they went dimmer. He didn't want to go in because it was misty and gloomy. He eventually went in and he looked around but he couldn't see anybody or anything, apart from some torn clothes on the floor.

Then, as Peter was about to go out, he heard something in the trees rattling. He looked up and he just saw a white cat. He was then just about to pick up the clothes, when something moved in the corner of his eye. He went over, when a cat jumped out of the tree and ran away. He then turned around and there was a very strong werewolf. Peter ran out of the cemetery and turned round but there was nothing there.

So every night, Peter walks next to the cemetery, he sees the werewolf but it disappears.

Jamie Ross (13)

The Winter's Night

It was a dark winter's night, the roads were icy and the bare trees swayed in the strong wind.

My dad was driving along a long snake-like road, when he saw two hitchhikers. He stopped and wound down his window and as he was about to say, 'Get in!' he heard the sudden loud screech of car brakes. From out of nowhere one of the hitchhikers seemed to be hit by something and was knocked on to my dad's car bonnet and the other of the two men was knocked to the ground as though a car had hit him.

My dad jumped out of his car as quickly as he could and went to look at the bodies, but they weren't there and there was no blood. At the side of the road there was a gravestone that read: 'At this point at about ten o'clock on the twentieth of December 1985 two male hitchhikers were killed in an accident involving two cars'.

My dad was so shocked that he got in his car and sped along the long winding road and didn't stop until he got to his mum's house. When he got there it was just before twelve o'clock. As he got out of his car he heard a loud ear-piercing sound that seemed to come from above just like he had heard before, he looked up into the moonlit sky but he could see nothing except from the cold snowflakes falling to the frost-bitten ground.

He went inside and went up to bed and all that night he was wondering if he had been dreaming or whether he had seen the ghosts reliving their last moments of life!

Benjamin Jobson (13)

Dead Spells

It was a dark and gloomy night when a young boy went missing. For weeks on end there was a massive search party but he was never found again.

In hate the boy's mother turned from believing in God to believing in the Devil; but then as soon as she learned, she cast a cruel spell upon her son's death place. Over the years many people went missing. The old woman got the blame and a lot of abuse in the street.

She noticed a shadow at the end of her bed getting fainter and fainter. She heard her son say, 'I don't forgive you, so you shall live in the Underworld.'

Now you can still see her ghost walking around the eerie death spot of her son.

Jonathan Norris (13)

The Stalker

On a dark night there's a full moon and the stalker strikes. On a dark country lane. Screams from a young woman running away from the stalker who is hacking at the woman's husband.

One year later . . .

The full moon was out and two young men were going down the old country lane. They saw the abandoned Corsa in the middle of the lane. Then two men got out of their car and had a look in. The men were shocked to see the bones of a man in the car. All of a sudden they heard a thud on the car. It was the stalker!

The two jumped in the Corsa and drove off. The stalker fell off and hung on to the bumper. The two young men thought they were safe but the stalker crashed through the window and slit the driver's throat with a knife. The car spun out of control. Bill jumped out into the woods. Then he found a house in the woods.

His friend's head was hanging above the door with a puddle of blood below. The man went for a look in the house. The house was full of murder weapons. The stalker crept behind him and killed him with an axe.

Scott Brown (13)

The Screaming Sewer

One dark and stormy night there were two people, Fred Rumpert and Adam Sneezy, who were going down the road when they heard a screaming noise coming from the old abandoned railway underground. They thought they would check it out.

They walked towards the manhole where they would go down and suddenly the place got cold. The hairs on their neck stood on end. They slowly lifted up the manhole cover and a puff of foul-smelling steam rose up out of the hole.

They climbed down the slimy old ladder, then suddenly Adam slipped and brought Fred down with him. They fell with a big bang! The tunnel was like a hole that a worm would make. They continued down the tunnel to find that the ladder had been pulled down by someone or something! A cold chilling shudder ran down their arms and legs. They started hovering above the ground and moved closer to where the bellowing sounds were coming from.

Adam and Fred found that the screams were dead spirits trying to be freed from Hell! Further down the tunnel they heard music, music that curdled the blood! Suddenly their minds went blank and they fainted. They were never seen again, but the ghosts stayed there to haunt off other people, so their fates wouldn't be sealed like themselves!

The two boys are now said to wander where they used to walk! Screams are still heard coming from the old chilled manhole.

The end! Or is it . . .?

Iain Fawcett (12)

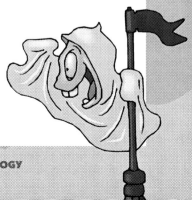

Drip, Drip, Drip

Timmy was the only child of the family. His parents couldn't have any more children. They bought him a puppy to play with instead.

Timmy had bunk beds fitted in his room so that the dog could lay on the bottom and every time Timmy felt scared or alone he'd just reach his hand down and let the dog lick it.

One night, when his parents were out there was a giant thunderstorm cutting off all the power in the house. Scared and frightened, he and his dog went to bed. As he was just going to sleep he heard this dripping sound. *Drip, drip, drip!* So he got out of bed and checked all the taps and pipes in the house (with the aid of his flashlight) and they were fine so he returned to bed, but still he heard the *drip, drip, drip!* So now scared, he reached his hand down and let the dog lick it, its tongue was more rough than usual, so he went out a checked the taps again. Still fine. As he entered his room the power returned and there, hanging from his lampshade hung his beloved dog 'dripping' with blood and on the wall, scrawled out in crimson-red transcribed, *'Humans can lick too!'* Then after a small breeze brushed passed him the light was once again drained from the room.

Mark Allison (13)

Saxon Curse

It was a hundred years ago in a dark, damp, candlelit house there lived three girls and their brothers.

It was a horrid night when they had just moved in. They had found out that it was built on an old Saxon village that was burned down by a jealous chief. The village was destroyed and all who lived there.

Every year on the 19th of August the chief's ghost rises and he looks for his revenge on whoever killed him and his people.

Every year the people who live in the house are forced to move or they die by the curse placed on it.

First you get strange messages and after that the house became unbearably cold. Next the house gets hot, very hot, just like when the house was originally burned down.

The day of the event and the house shakes violently and a voice says, 'Who killed me and my people?'

As you live in the house he thinks it was you. Then the house gets engulfed in ghostly flames. This lasts for twenty-four hours. The following morning the house's shell is fine, but as you proceed inside, all who inhabited it are dead!

Over the years all who died come back that night and try to battle with the Saxons but every year the Saxons defeat the other spectres.

All the spectres have to do to rest in peace is defeat the Saxons this will lift the curse.

The house in the story is the one we live in.

Kayleigh Thompson (12)

What Is Underneath

Jessica edged forward, 'Shall I go in?' she questioned.
'Yeah,' replied Carla, as she smirked.
'But everyone says this house is haunted by the young girl Louisa who was killed!'
'Poppycock,' shouted Carla. 'Just go in and look where they say she is buried in the front room. What could go wrong?'
'What could go right you mean,' Jessica mumbled under her breath.
The two girls edged over the passage of the big old house and entered the room carefully.

The door creaked and a light vanilla fragrance filled the air.
'Oh that smells beautiful,' cried Jessica.
'I'm not sure about this Jessica, it's too creepy,' said Carla doubtfully.
'It was your idea in the first place,' Jessica replied.
'Yeah, well I was only trying to get you more popular at school.'
'Oh well in that ca . . .'
Just at that moment the door slammed tight shut and the only light in the room was from a small slit in the wall shaped like an 'L'. It landed on a space in the floor where a loose floorboard was sticking up slightly.
Carla tried the door, it was locked tight.

Jessica raced over to the slit and started screaming, 'Help!'
Carla joined her.
Suddenly three loose floorboards flew up and hit Jessica on the back and twice on the head knocking her unconscious.

Carla screamed as a skeleton not much bigger than her jumped up and . . .

Nobody ever saw or found the two girls again.

So what was underneath?

Laura Allen (13)

The Ghost

The house was very dark but, I didn't need any light. In the corridor, there was mud and soil on the ground, there was also the odd cobweb. (Cleaning isn't my forte.)

One day, I was just looking around and remembering the past. Then I heard footsteps and then a big bang, that was the front door. Then I looked over the balcony and I saw lots of shadows. My long dress trailed behind me as I went downstairs.

I went into the kitchen, where the people were, I picked up a rolling pin, which was on the wall on my left. I lifted it above my head for security.

Unexpectedly, they turned and I screamed as loud as I could. When I had stopped, there was a slight pause, then they ran out of the house screaming, 'Ghost!'

Erin Taylor (11)

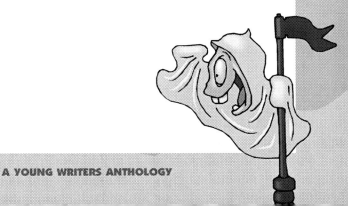

The Haunted Staircase

A nearby house had a staircase that was decidedly haunted. So I went to this house.

When I entered, there was silence. My hostess asked me whether I would like her to show me the haunted staircase. A few months ago she had been pushed down the staircase by invisible hands. She warned me never, under any circumstances, to go up these stairs. When I asked why, she just said 'You see, there is something at the top of the stairs always waiting.'

In spite of what I had been told, I was intrigued and decided to make an attempt to climb the staircase alone. It was midnight; the house was silent. I felt alone, not only in the house but in the whole world. As I made my way up the staircase, it seemed I was being followed. I was probably being silly, so I carried on my way up the stairs. I stopped for a moment and felt breathing on my neck. Then my nostrils were filled with a sweet, slightly sickly smell. I was so frightened I descended the stairs. When I reached the bottom, I returned to my room. I felt like a coward. My fright had won me over, but looking back I'm glad I did. I never want to know what was at the top of the stairs!

Nicole Carman (14)

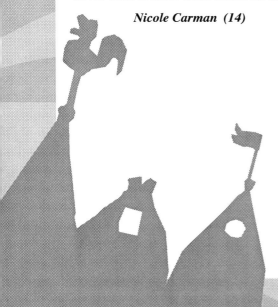

A Dream

One day I was alone. The house was empty, just me alone. I was about to go to bed when I heard a sound. It was like someone screaming. I couldn't catch the sound. I heard it again. This time it sounded like 'Help me!' That's what I heard.

I started to get goose bumps, my brain froze. 'Help me!' The sound kept on going on and on in my head. I started to sense that fear was in me, Josh Mannix, the king. I began to sense that someone had been killed in my house. I needed help, my house was haunted.

I started to walk downstairs. The staircase seemed to get longer as did the voice. My ear drums were bursting and thumping. The room got bigger and bigger. The ghost was pale. Her face was small and her body was big. I ran back up the stairs and reached the bathroom and locked myself inside. I seemed to be there for ages.

I unlocked the bathroom door slowly. There she was, right in front of me. I screamed my loudest. She covered my mouth, sat down beside me and started to talk to me. An alarm word. It was my alarm clock. I woke up - it seemed real but it was a dream.

Josh Mannix (12)

Jail Boy

58, 59, 60...
Two days and I'm out of solitary confinement. One person. That's it. I only killed one. She deserved it. She stole my only son. He was mine as much as he was hers and to think I loved her before.

This place stinks and I have to spend two years in here. But it's better than normal cells. I can't imagine a cell with weird people I don't know.

What was that?
I felt something cold...
Who called me?

It's her! She's come back to haunt me. She hates me... I hate her more. There she is. She has a knife. Help me someone!

'Guard! Help me! Guard!'

No one's answering me; they think I'm mad.

Noooo! Gone. Just like that! No! It's still cold. She's still here and she's still calling me. But it's a different voice!

No... she took the child!

Toby Burraway (12)

Scary Waters

Mark and Kim were packing their bags. They were going camping on Carry Island for a few nights.

'Where's Charlie?' asked Kim.
'I think he's outside in the boat waiting for us,' replied Mark
'Right so we've got all the stuff' said Kim.

3:30. It was time they were leaving. They went down to the boat.
'Charlie, here boy' shouted Kim. As Charlie ran down the drive he lost his collar but they did not notice.

They were half way across the sea, heavy storms came. The sky turned grey and big waves came. As they drove more into the sea the storm got worse. Then the boat started to rock and then it happened. The boat capsized. As they were falling they were caught by something. Then they heard calming music, which seemed to die out slowly. Something stood them up on top of the water and they were able to walk across the water, to Carry Island, so they thought.

They must have fallen asleep while floating on top of the water, but never sinking. During the night the current must have turned them around but it still looked as if they were heading towards Carry Island. So as they lay on the water they were really heading towards their home on the beach. As they became closer they became very excited and they fell through the water. They were washed up on the beach. When they woke up, for all they knew it was a dream. Or was it?

Lauren Allen (13)

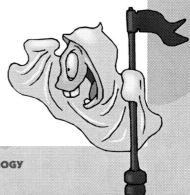

The Den In The Haunted House

Oliver, Mark and me were bored playing football, so we decided to explore the old house on top of the hill that was haunted.

When we found it we were a bit scared to go inside. When we tried the door it wouldn't open, but then we saw a little window open and because I was the smallest, we thought I could get in.

I was really scared and it was small and I got stuck but they pushed me through and I opened the door quick. It wasn't so scary inside so we decided to make a den because nobody would go near a haunted house.

We found some old wood and put it over the windows so that nobody could see us. It was very dark and we needed some light but the door couldn't open and the window had blown shut. We thought something was going to get us but Oliver found the light on his key ring and we managed to find the window handle.

I went through the window head first and kicked the door and it flew open and then they ran out. When we looked up at the chimney we could see lots of birds flying in and out so that must have been the noise.

We shut the door and decided that when we went back next time we would make sure we took our torches.

William Tate (13)

Sweet Dreams

Mary was on her third glass of punch. It was her prom night. A night she would never forget. She was talking to Todd, a quarterback on the school's football team. Just then her best friend Jenny burst in and drew out a revolver! Jenny spotted Kate Miller the leading cheerleader, a real snob. Jenny aimed the revolver at Kate and shot her right through the heart. Kate stumbled backwards into the wall and slid to the floor. You could see blood trickling down her! Kate Miller was dead!

Jenny then spotted Todd, her ex-boyfriend with Mary her best friend. Mary of all people. Well she'd soon put a stop to this! Jenny then aimed the revolver at Todd and shot. Luckily she missed them. Mary and Todd ran outside and hid in a large group of trees near the school, but Jenny soon tracked them down like a hungry wolf running through the trees chasing after them both like a mad thing! She was unstoppable.

Jenny shot again. This time it was more than once, several bullets heading towards them. They ran into a wall, it was a dead end! First she shot Todd one blow right through the head. Todd was dead. Next it was Mary's turn! It went right through her neck. A few seconds later Mary was dead too! Mary woke up it was all a dream, a silly little dream or was it!

Angharad Seabury (13)

Lord Townby Vs Lady Townby

'Lady Townby was never seen again.' Katie McCalm said in a spooky whisper.

Lady Townby also lived in Quarndon Hall. She was strolling in her grounds. Meanwhile, one of her maids was doing some cooking in the scullery when she heard a bloodcurdling scream. The maid, along with the rest of the household all ran outside. All of a sudden, dull, black clouds came over the bright, blue sky. Thunder started rumbling whilst raging lightning began to flash. So the scream was drowned by the nightmarish tempest.

The McCalms were distant relatives to the Townbys. Katie was having a sleepover with her friends, they were sleeping in the attic. The weather was just like eighty years ago when Lady Townby went missing.

At that moment there was a groan of the floorboards, the girls screamed with terror. The door crashed open, it was Sophie, Katie's big sister. 'I feel sorry for you kids,' she said, ''cause tonight is the night when Lady Townby comes back to, well, visit.' She gave a frightful scream and ran downstairs. The girls went to sleep. Smash, bang, scream, wicked laugh. The girls woke with a fright. Lady Townby was floating in mid-air.

'Time for revenge.' she cried, pulling out a knife. The girls ran into the garden. Standing there was Lord Townby.

'Don't force me to do it' he said sternly.

'Don't' replied Lady Townby. The Lord opened a box, they both fell into it.

Clare McLoughlin (11)

The Ghost Story

Soon after midnight, three boys called Jack, Tom and George went to an old, spooky looking house.

The three boys were very sensible and intelligent so they hesitated and didn't go in straight away.

Tom, Jack and George went into the nasty looking house. At this point, Tom and George wanted to go back but they decided not to and then people kept jumping out on them. They were terrified but they still kept walking, all the lights went off and they were crying their heads off.

They were kicking at the walls and then heard a *bang, bang*, it was coming from the right of them. It was really near and then the lights came on just in time. They went right near the door. The door came open and they went out and they were there a year trying to find their way out and that's how it ended.

Jordan Rutherford (9)

A Night In The Adersons' House

'Be quiet it's twelve o'clock at night, the landlord will hear you,' said Kimmy.
'Oh stop moaning we're nearly there,' I said.
'Where are we going anyway? *Where are we going?'*
'Oh my God Sammy it's a ghost!'
'Oh nnooo,' I screamed.
'Please don't run away, I mean don't do that!' bellowed the ghost.
'Do what?' said Kimmy.
'Confuse me like that,' said the ghost.
'Sorry, come on Kimmy,' I said.
'You didn't answer my question,' said Kimmy.

The kitchens.
'I'm starving,' I said.
'You woke me up for that, I'm going back to bed,' said Kimmy grumpily.
'Oh please don't go I'm scared,' I said shakily.

She walked away. I stood there in the darkness when suddenly this unearthly cry filled the house. There was a narrow staircase to my right, it sounded like the cry was coming from there. I ran to the top, curiosity getting the better of me. I slowly opened the door and slipped inside. The room I was standing in was filled with jewels and dressed. In the far corner was the ghost I had seen a couple of hours ago. I said, 'Can I help you?'
'Yes you can,' wailed the ghost.
'How?' I asked.
'You could find a portal.'

'Well there was this big, twirly gateway near my room,' I said.
'Brilliant, let's go.'

A few hours later, we found my room and the portal.

'Well goodbye,' said the ghost.
'Wake up, wake up,' said Kimmy.
'Cool night last night,' I said.
'What are you talking about?' said Kimmy.
'You mean you don't remember meeting the ghost?' I said.
'No and hurry up we're going to miss the bus.' said Kimmy.

Stephanie Hennerbry

The Haunted House

Ryan, Jake, Virag and me went camping in the moonlight when we dared to go in the haunted house. We all went out.

'*Rooogghh*' we all heard, it was a wolf howling. We saw a shadow as we were still creeping to the house.

Jake opened the door. The creak of the door made my spine shiver. Bats flew in all of our faces, then we saw a coffin creak open. It was a mummy. We all ran. Then I saw a zombie. We ran upstairs. While we were pushing all of the cobwebs out of the way, we pushed a door and locked it. We heard a funny noise. We turned slowly but before we knew it, there was a vampire. We all quickly undid the door and rushed out. The floor was rumbling, we fell down the tall stairs with a *thud*. The mummy was free. He started to strangle Ryan but his head fell off. I unwrapped his bandage and then he fell, dead.

We ran fast but Jake fell down the bottomless pit. Then I saw Frankenstein with a gun. He shot me in the leg. He was about to shoot me in the head, when Buffy staked him. Then I jumped out against the dazzling light. I saw Jake, Ryan and Virag.

James McKenzie (9)

The Scare!

I was going to my friend's house to watch a scary movie and we started to hear footsteps so Lucy got a knife, Jody got a rolling pin, Palu got a saw from the shed and Andrew got the drill. We went upstairs and had a look around but there was nothing there.
'Oh where are the noises coming from, it wasn't me'
'Or me,'
'Or me,'
'Shut up, just try to see if you can find him.'
'This house is haunted,' said Lucy terrifyingly.

As we were talking, the man ran from the closet to the window. They turned around and saw him so Palu and Andrew went downstairs and chased him off but he had already gone.
'Oh damn,' said Palu scaredly. So they sat down and watched the movie and the floor started to rumble.
'Oh no, what are we going to do?'
'I don't know.'
'Oh no, it's starting to fall through.'

'Where are we?'
'Ahh cool we're undergound.'
'Look there is an air vent we could go through it,' said Palu excitedly.

It led us to the park, from where we walked home and got indoors and it was a terrible sight. I could not believe it, one of the settees was gone.

We had to go home and it left Lucy on her own. That night she heard a noise coming from the attic so she called the police and they arrested him.

Courtney Green (9)

A House

Then I found myself running down a long hallway and there at the end of the hallway was a huge door beautifully carved with diamond shapes cut into it.

I ran for it, it seemed like the only place I could hide at the time, I touched the golden door handle, it was ice-cold. Suddenly everything went cold and from my mouth I blew out a cloud of cold air, someone or something was behind the door. There was nowhere else I could go so I started turning the handle, my body freezing. I stepped in, there were old statues everywhere but there was no one there. The statues were covered in cobwebs which glistened in the light. I looked through the window, the stars were beautiful, it looked like someone had dropped a million gems or crystals over a black sheet.

I awoke to hanging noises, I ran outside, it all went cold again and this face appeared in the wall. A hand reached out, it almost had me but something was pulling me back, it was also ice-cold, I was pulled forward again, it just wouldn't let go. I was getting pulled in then it disappeared. I got up and turned around, nothing was there. I ran down the hallway, threw myself down the stairs and ran out the door.
    I started up my car and drove off.
    What was holding my hand?
    Why did it save me?
    I'll never forget that day.

Samantha Short (11)

The House On Cherry Hill

The house on Cherry Hill in Texas, California had been locked up for 302 years and had been well-known for its sleek looks and sly mysteries! Here's a story that will really make you tingle!

Mary and her father John wanted to make a clean start so they decided to move to Texas. They opened the big door of the big house and Mary walked into the house and she started exploring it.

Later that night, when both Mary and her father were asleep, Mary heard strange noises.

'Who's there?' She grabbed an old bottle for protection and she got out of her hard bed and started looking around. All of a sudden, she was pushed back to the hallway and she smacked the walls! 'He's out there
... Run!'

All of a sudden Mary ran out of the house and was never seen again!

Charlotte Bebbington (11)

Jasper The Funny Ghost

Rolling down the old staircase, Jasper the funny ghost got up and drifted over towards the kitchen. He stuffed his face with custard cream cakes, just to realise that it had all fallen on the floor in a heap (it had gone right through him). Grandfather ghost was coming into the hall, Jasper hurriedly hid in the cereal cupboard until he was gone. He floated into the study and turned on the TV, just as *Ghostwatch* was coming on. A mad ghost on the run from jail, apparently tried to freeze his ghostly figure into a statue so that he wouldn't get caught again. He failed. 'This was boring,' thought Jasper, 'I want to have some fun.'

He went outside into the garden and played *Swing the Ghost* on a rope hanging out of a tree. He was terribly hungry, but he couldn't eat food because it went right through him. It was getting dark now. Jasper went inside and decided to play some tricks on Mama ghost. She was coming up the hall now. Jasper floated out in front of her and went 'Boooo!'
Bad idea, he got grounded for two days, just for that, it was so unfair. Jasper thought, about being cooped up inside the manor for 48 hours but it wouldn't be so bad, would it?

Lisa Telford (11)

Bottled Out

Five boys were walking in the woods to find a dare to initiate two of them, Paul and Andrew, into their gang. They saw an abandoned, spooky-looking cottage so they dared Paul and Andrew into it. They were really frightened but went inside.
'I want to go home,' cried Andrew.
Suddenly Paul screamed to Andrew, 'Look behind you.'
There were three white, pale human bodies making funny sounds, but Paul and Andrew were too scared to scream so they panicked. Andrew grabbed an old poker from beside the hearth and threw it at one of the zombie's heads, but missed. The zombie laughed and pulled his mask off his face; it was one of the gang. They had been playing a trick to scare Paul and Andrew.
Paul asked, 'Are we in the gang now?'
Yeah,' they said, 'but we'll have to check around first.'
So they all went into the kitchen. There was rusty old range. Standing on it was a bottle with some white powder in the bottom. Andrew pulled the cork out and there was a sudden puff of smoke, and when it cleared there was a skeleton clacking towards them. The skeleton shrieked, and roared 'Now it's your turn to share your destiny in this bottle.'

The terrified gang ran for their lives to the front door but it was now bolted. If you ever walk in the woods and come across a little cottage with a range and a bottle in it, *don't take the cork out!*

Richard Gilbert (9)

Help!

Rachel and Charlotte walked in the mist, Rachel stood out because she had smooth, blonde hair, but Charlotte had dark hair. They both had one thing in common they were both sensitive. Their eyes were brown and lips were pink. They both had white skin and it was smooth. The mist flowed in their faces, they couldn't see anything - until - they saw it - the house. The haunted one they saw on the news. They looked at each other frightened and decided to go in. They went to open the door, but before they could get the chance it fell down. Charlotte crept in first, then Rachel - but as soon as they walked in 'Help,' they both cried.

They'd fallen from up to underground.
'Ouch!' Rachel moaned.
'Be quiet, I can hear something,' hissed Charlotte. Her voice echoed through the undergrowth.
'What can you hear?' whispered Rachel.
'Shhh.'
'Ahh, whooooooooo, ahhhhhhhhh,' cried what sounded like a spirit. Then they froze as it came into view, it was a pitch-black, but it was so gruesome, you could still see it. It looked like a killer, killer monster. Suddenly a see-through, creamy thing flew over their heads.
'Please help,' they squealed. Charlotte had an idea she saw steps leading out. Rachel saw a light, she switched it on, it scared the monster, it got dizzy and ran away. They ran and ran until they were back home. But - they daren't - tell their mums.

Rachel Chilcott (9)

Hardlock House

Faye and I saw an enormous, creaky door. As we went on we saw a huge, long hallway that felt very gloomy. There were spooky family pictures on the wall. As we stepped on the creaky floorboards we spotted a skeleton and bloodstained carpet. Then we heard ghostly screams from the gloomy staircase.

As we got to the top of the stairs we heard a bony hand tapping annoyingly on the bloodstained windows. I ran down the stairs and got out, but Faye said, 'It's the water going through the pipes of the central heating.'

The ghost and skeleton chased Faye. Then the door opened and Faye fell in some dirt. We went safely home. But that wasn't the end of Hardlock House. The spookies are still up and about, but it was the end of us - we never went to that place again.

Jodi Riggan (8)

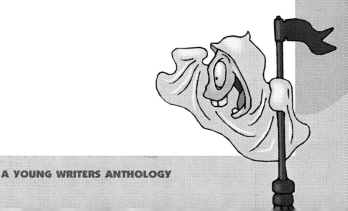

Information

We hope you have enjoyed reading this book - and that you will continue to enjoy it in the coming years.

If you like reading and writing drop us a line, or give us a call, and we'll send you a free information pack.

<u>Write To</u>

**Young Writers Information
Remus House
Coltsfoot Drive
Woodston
Peterborough
PE2 9JX
(01733) 890066**